# Goodnight Irene

By

James Scott Byrnside

# ACKNOWLEDGMENTS

I would like to thank Mary Brennan, Alexandra Johns, Shelly Woods, Meredith Tennant and Jaimie-Lee Wise for their invaluable assistance.

A list of all the people who encouraged me would be quite long. Suffice it to say, you know who you are.

Cover artwork and design by Matt Willis-Jones

For information, contact: sbyrnside@gmail.com

# CONTENTS

This novel is dedicated to Christianna Brand. She was not the most prolific or celebrated mystery writer. She was the best.

James Scott Byrnside

# PROLOGUE

# CHICAGO 1907

Dorothy Roberts rang up Pop Morse' Roadhouse. Pop Morse said that everyone had split; the place had gone dark.

"Robert Lasciva? Tall, handsome, a real bimbo…"

"Yeah, I know the guy. He left already. Everybody left already. I told you." Pop's asthmatic wheeze hissed over the silence.

"Did he say where he was going?"

Pop got tired of the whole business and ended the conversation with a click of the receiver.

Dorothy tried the Brown Bear and Smalleys but everyone had finished for the night. She clawed through the gravelly debris at the bottom of her purse and scrounged a dull penny.

*One last coin but there's nowhere left to call.*

She held it in front of the slot for a moment. Her fingers went limp and the coin fell back into a pile of lint and make-up.

*Where the hell is he? He might have gone back to my apartment. Irene is asleep, snug as a bug in a rug. He'll wake her.*

She furrowed her brow at the thought and attempted to roll a cigarette in the booth. Snowflakes drifted through the splintered wood and suffused the tiny paper, turning the tobacco to mush. Dorothy let out an irked huff of breath and clenched her bony hand into a fist. She held this pose until her fingernails penetrated her palm, then dropped the mangled ball of tobacco onto the slush.

The door frame jostled open and Dorothy gingerly heel-toed the sheet of ice covering the ground. As she shivered down Fullerton Avenue, a cacophony of stray dog barks punctured the silent Chicago night. Chimney smoke billowed out from countless rooftops and drifted toward the heavens before dissolving into the starless, stony sky.

"Dorothy!" The voice bellowed from the second story of a familiar old brownstone. Alice Schmidt hung her upper torso out of the window and rested her swollen arms on the ledge. Her sharp, staccato voice emanated from her rosebud mouth, centered by perpetually flushed cheeks. "Dorothy, what are you doing?" Alice's German accent rendered 'Dorothy' as 'Dorozee' and 'what' as 'vaht.'

"I needed to get out. I was going batty in the apartment, just needed to walk around."

"Is Irene home alone?" Alice had a way of turning her questions into accusations.

"Irene is in bed. She's fine, really. When I left, she was snoring. She snores just like her father did."

"I know." Alice left her mouth open.

The two women stared in silence. Dorothy waited for Alice to say something else. She would have continued waiting but her scalp began to freeze from all the snow piled into her hair. The warm vapor of her breath brushed against the insensate tip of her nose.

"Irene is fine."

"Do you want to come in? You can have some tea and get warm."

Irritation crept into Dorothy's voice. "No, I should get back and check on Irene. If she wakes up, she'll start crying and she'll be all alone. What kind of mother would I be? Who leaves their child home alone? Who does a thing like that?"

Alice leaned her head out the window. "Be sure to tell the little mäuschen I will see her on Monday. Yes?"

"Of course. It's her favorite thing in the world."

"And if she's awake when you get home, tell her Alice said, 'Goodnight, Irene.'"

"Goodnight, Alice."

"Auf wiedersehen." She held her pudgy arms aloft and shut the window.

*She's right. What are you doing? You got all dressed up. For what? It doesn't matter. Don't ask. Just move. One step, two steps down the street. No other thoughts now.*

The front door to the town home bulldozed the accumulated snow and Dorothy stepped into the vestibule. It reeked of the downtrodden and tobacco. She rolled a cigarette with her stubby fingers and finally inhaled the calming smoke. The numb slowly left her face as she looked through the dirt-stained window at her neighborhood, blanketed in white.

*This city is gorgeous if you don't have to live in it.*

Her thoughts, like the flakes in the air, drifted waywardly. Eventually they found their way to memories of the past. The images were awash with a serene luminosity that contrasted painfully with the present tense of her life.

The visions of her old apartment came easily. The sunlight shone through the window and covered the living room like honey. Dust particles flitted visibly in the brilliant beams of light. Dorothy carried Irene around the room and told her about every face in every photograph on the wall. Harold leaned back in the chair, his pipe firmly held in the corner of his mouth. He adjusted it and the stem clicked against his teeth. The sound brought with it the other senses.

In September of 1903, the roof caved in. Harold's nose began to bleed several times a day. It frightened Dorothy but Harold ignored it. One night, she noticed bumps on his chest. They resembled rotten cherries and felt knotty to the touch. Something was wrong. She pleaded with him to go to the hospital but he refused. One morning he defecated green liquid and Dorothy called a doctor. By then it was too late. The only solace was that Irene had not contracted typhoid as well.

And now…

*Snap out of it. Where are you? You're at home and… Irene. If Robert came, he probably knocked a few times and left. I hope she didn't answer the door. She's all alone up there. She's so little.*

She flicked the half-smoked cigarette into the dark corner. As Dorothy watched its smoldering tip dissipate, a panic grew in her gut. She paced the tiny corridor and the images in her mind coalesced into grotesque montages.

*Move.*

Heels in hand, she bounded up the stairs toward the seventh floor. During one manic leap, the slippery silk of her stocking threw her off balance and her knees landed on the top of a riser. Her scream echoed up and down the stairwell. No one answered it. With wobbling legs and heaving breath, she picked herself up and limped to her floor.

A thin shaft of light poured out of Dorothy's apartment, piercing the blackness of the hall. She stood across from it, rubbing her aching

5

knees.

*Oh, no.*

As Dorothy hobbled along the hallway, the darkened walls seemed to be collapsing on her. She stopped in front of her door and ran her hand along the splintered wood. The smell of alcohol wafted through the crack. Her trembling index finger pushed the door open.

Jack Tellum sat at the kitchen table holding a cloth to his thumb and looking gruff. The white fabric was spotted with red. A revolver sat perched in his shoulder holster. Robert's nickname for Jack was 'Toad' because his head and neck moved as a solitary unit with only a double chin to show any separation.

He regarded her without expression.

"Where's Robert?" Dorothy asked.

The toad's lack of expression remained and he said nothing.

"Robert. Robert!" Her voice cracked under the strain of the volume.

Jack finally spoke. "Easy now, don't lose your lovely head over this."

Dorothy inched to the bedroom door, keeping her eyes on the man at the table. "My daughter, Irene… She was here all alone. I need to make sure she's safe."

"Yeah, well, that's reasonable. Just don't lose it. Not now." Tellum offered the barest hint of a smile.

An ache started at the back of Dorothy's eyes and her mouth moved without saying anything. Her hand blindly twisted the knob. She turned toward the bed and the tension left her body. What little color there was, drained away from her brittle cheeks. Her eyes slewed toward the full-length mirror in the corner of the room and she saw herself cracked by the glass. Then, as if in a trance, Dorothy Roberts walked out of the bedroom window into mid-air and landed on the ice, seven floors below.

# CHAPTER 1

# CHICAGO 1927

"The time is almost upon us."

Rowan Manory put away his pocket watch and rolled a cigarette under an elm tree. The detective was a stocky box of a man with a black suit featuring wide notch lapels that nearly covered his shoulders. He pushed the cigarette into the corner of his mouth.

His assistant, Walter Williams, opted to stand under the sun. Walter was a tall, lanky man, with a thin jazz suit, tinged the slightest possible shade of grey. He inhaled the sublime scent of spring as it breezed through Chicago's affluent South Shore neighborhood. "Isn't it grand, Manory?"

"You are referring to this neighborhood?" Rowan looked over the row of houses.

"No, I mean the season. Hope springing eternal, the butterflies, the squirrels, and the rejuvenation of life—that sort of thing."

Rowan struck a match and puffed the cigarette to life. "For every one homicide during the fall and winter, there are three in spring and summer. It is not only the flora and fauna that flourish with the thaw. There is also the rebirth of the sisters, animus and avarice. They seem to be fanatical about warm weather."

Walter nodded. "You must admit the squirrels are adorable. Look at them, chasing each other up the tree."

Rowan could not suppress his smile. "Are you mocking me, Williams?"

Walter held out his thumb and index finger a few inches apart. "Just a little bit. I think one can enjoy a picturesque day without dwelling on humanity's moral turpitude."

"That is completely dependent on one's point of view. Now, Williams, before we enter the house, let us go over everything we know thus far."

"We haven't even talked to the client yet."

"Yes, but the story has dominated the newspapers for the last three weeks. We know some basic facts. Tell them to me."

Walter joined Rowan in the shade and pulled out his notepad. "The victim was Martin Brent, proprietor of Brent Real Estate and Loan. He was murdered on the second of March."

"Who were the last people to see Mr. Brent alive?"

"His seven employees. According to their statements, Brent entered his office just before four o'clock p.m. and locked the door. At that point, they went home for the evening, leaving him alone in the building."

Rowan looked down the street in both directions. "The building is nearby?"

Walter pointed to the left. "It's on Langley and Phillips, about fifteen minutes on foot. It's an isolated little cul-de-sac, but there are two separate alleys leading into it, making it easily accessible."

"Very good. Continue."

"At about a quarter past five, the cleaning service showed up. It was three men – two Poles and a Czech. The names are Marcin Woj…" Walter stared at the page for a moment. "I'm not going to try and pronounce the names. They discovered the body and notified the police."

"How did they discover the body?"

"The door to Martin Brent's office was still locked, but the inside of the room was visible through the window. The victim was hunched over his desk with piano wire around his neck. Nothing was stolen. His keys were found in a trash can around the corner."

"And what does this tell us?"

Walter shrugged. "The killer may have been a pianist?"

"Do your parents know how brilliant you are?"

He grinned. "Yeah, they have a pretty good idea."

"This tells us that Mr. Brent probably knew his killer, at least enough to unlock the office door for him. It tells us that this was a crime of passion or long-term gain. Most importantly, it gives us a solid time frame for the murder. Barring some extraordinary case of collusion, Brent's employees and those of the cleaning service have alibis and no apparent motive."

"That's correct. The only people who stand to benefit from his death are the wife, Agatha, and the brother, Tommy. The brother was recently added to the will, but he won't receive anything substantial. Agatha is the primary beneficiary. She gave birth three weeks before the murder and has been housebound since that time. At the time of the murder, she was at home taking care of the baby. According to her statement, Tommy Brent was with her from three forty-five until five o'clock."

"So, they have provided one another with an alibi."

"Well, there's always the love triangle possibility. She could be covering for Tommy."

Rowan blew out a ring of smoke. "Agatha Brent hired us because she is discouraged at the lack of progress by the police. That does not strike me as particularly suspicious. If she had been involved in the murder of her husband, I doubt she would have hired a private detective."

"Tommy may have paid someone to kill his brother, but he's a dewdropper."

Rowan gave Walter a look of disappointment. "Please use English when speaking to me."

"The man's a leech. He hasn't had a steady job since... well, since forever. He moved in to help with the baby and, presumably, to eat the food. That would make him a logical suspect."

Rowan faced the Brent house at the end of the street. "The police thought he was the best suspect."

"They had Tommy in for questioning. They held him as long as they could, but like I said, he's covered for the duration of the time frame. There's no evidence to link him to the crime."

"We shall see." Rowan flicked the cigarette onto the grass and stomped it out. "The police have one other idea. During the last hour of his life, Martin Brent bought out a tractor company in Atlanta. The purchase was proposed and finalized at a quarter after four. The only people who knew about it were Martin and the owner of the company. The police believe the killer was in the office at the time of the sale and now plans to purchase the company after the case dies down. They are keeping this information under wraps."

"How do you know?"

"Inspector Grady is one of my few remaining friends with the police. He worked with my mother when she was on the force. Occasionally, he tips me off."

"That's awfully nice of him."

Rowan cast a sardonic glance. "The information is told when the information is sold. The police are looking into some competing firms and business rivals, but nothing has turned up as yet."

Rowan pulled out his pocket watch again and pulled the crown into the setting position. His thumb and forefinger twirled the dial back and forth, repositioning the hands.

*Past, present, and future.*

A smug smile appeared on his face. "It is time. Let us begin, Williams."

The detectives made their way up the front walkway of the Brent house. Rowan reached forward and took hold of a large doorknocker affixed to a gargoyle's mouth. He brought it down lightly on the door in two precise knocks.

After waiting a few seconds, Walter spun toward Rowan with wide eyes. He whispered, "Manory."

"What is it, Williams?"

"Is it 'Miss Brent' or 'Mrs. Brent'? Which honorific does one use for a widow?"

Rowan whispered, "Mrs."

Walter narrowed his eyes. "Are you sure? Technically, the woman still has the man's name. However, she's not legally married to him."

"For us it is not a question of legality, but rather intent. 'Mrs.' is used when the widow is devastated at the death of her husband and mourns his loss. If the woman is happy to be rid of the man, the correct term is 'Miss'. Do you recall Amanda Green?"

"The one with the legs?"

"Yes, the woman who had two legs."

"I remember her well."

"She was a 'Miss'."

Tommy Brent opened the door. His wild eyes appeared to be in constant dilation. When speaking, he revealed small teeth buried in large gums. "Well, how about this, two dicks for the price of one. Wow."

Rowan's mouth moved without saying anything.

"Well, don't just stand there like a couple fancy pants scarecrows. Come on in." Tommy pushed the door wide, beckoning them forward.

They entered the hall and Walter shut the door.

Tommy Brent's head was pencil-thin with hair sprouting from the top in all directions. "Now, don't go telling me. Let me guess." He pointed his finger and moved it like a pendulum from Rowan to Walter and back again. He stopped at Rowan. "You're Rowan Manory. You're the main man."

Rowan arched his eyebrows. "That is correct."

"You know how I knew?"

"No."

"I'm a superior judge of character. I can tell by the way the other fellow is just a little bit behind you."

"Well done, Mr. Brent. This is my assistant, Walter Williams."

Walter extended his hand and Tommy clutched it like a lifeline at sea.

"Charmed, I'm sure." Tommy stood back and exhaled. "So you are real life, honest-to-God, private eyes?"

Rowan began to speak but Tommy interrupted him.

"What kind of gun do you carry?"

Rowan said, "We do not carry firearms."

Tommy snorted. "Well that's just silly. What happens when a bad man points a gun at you?"

Rowan put his hand on Walter's shoulder. "In the occurrence of such an event, Williams dazzles the criminal with his boundless wit."

Tommy eyed Walter. "Are you really that witty?"

Walter nodded. "Yes. Yes, I am."

They walked down the hall toward two closed sliding doors. Crystal figurines of angels, fairies, and demons littered the shelves along the walls.

Tommy stopped in front of the doors and faced the detectives. "Now, Agatha, she's not in her right mind. You need to know that going in." He placed a hand in his forest of hair and scratched. "The girl's been

16

through a lot. Try not to say anything too upsetting. Be gentle is what I'm saying. She's uhhh…" His forehead contracted. "What's the word I'm looking for?"

"Frail?" said Rowan.

"Fragile?" said Walter.

"Mental. The girl has gone mental. She's not thinking straight. And she's weak. The poor thing hasn't got much of an appetite."

Rowan said, "I will be most conscientious."

Tommy nodded and pulled the doors open.

Agatha Brent sat on the sofa with pale, languid, sunken cheeks. Her arms lay loose on her lap and her eyes looked in an undetermined direction, a convalescent glaze covering them.

The room had a large opened window overlooking the side lawn with thin, lacy curtains that rippled from the breeze. A wide fireplace lay dormant against the back wall. On the mantel there were several framed photographs and an art deco clock surrounded by jagged, natural red stone. At both far ends of the mantel, a crystal cherub prayed.

Rowan eased next to her on the couch. He looked into her blank eyes for a few seconds and then gently took her hand. "Mrs. Brent, words cannot accurately express my sympathy for your loss. You must know that I will not rest until your husband receives justice."

Tommy and Walter silently positioned themselves next to the

window.

Agatha's eyes did their best to focus on Rowan. "That's very kind." She spoke in a dreamy monotone. "Everyone has been so very kind. I just want this to end." She turned to Tommy with a pallid stare. "We both need to put this behind us, but it keeps dragging on and on like the worst kind of nightmare." Her head swayed back to Rowan. "That's why I called you, Mr. Manory. You come highly recommended."

"We will do our utmost to bring this case to a swift conclusion, I can assure you. Though I know it is painful for you, I have a few questions. I will be brief." He snapped his fingers and Walter pulled out his notebook. "Did your husband ever mention anyone who had issues with him – financial, personal, or otherwise? Did he have any outstanding debts?"

She formed the tired beginning of a smile, her lips barely rising. "Martin helped old people cross the street."

Rowan waited for her to continue but that was apparently all she was going to say. "You mean…"

She cleared her throat. "I mean he was beloved by everyone who knew him. No one had any reason to do this."

"No debts, though?"

"None that I know of."

"Why did Martin go to work so late in the day?"

"After Danny was born, Martin tried to stay home as much as

possible. That was difficult for him. He was always a hard-worker. Sometimes he would hold Danny and I would hold the phone for him." Agatha pretended to hold a phone to Rowan's head. "Like a team." She bent over with a silent laugh and took her time coming back up.

From the window, Tommy said, "My brother went to his office a few hours each day. He'd try and time the thing just right. When the boy was asleep he'd creep off to work for a bit and make sure everything was going okay and then slip back."

Rowan said, "Mrs. Brent, the day of the murder, what were you doing?"

She had told the police the details many times. "Danny went to sleep in the afternoon. I was exhausted and took the opportunity to get some sleep myself. I don't know what time it was; the clock in my room is broken. Some time later, I heard Danny crying. I went to the nursery and carried him to the living room. Tommy was on the sofa. He was reading a book."

Tommy said, "When the boy was born, I moved in to help out around the house."

Walter jotted down notes and Tommy glanced over his shoulder to see what he was writing.

Agatha said, "I saw the clock." She pointed toward the mantel. "It was ten till four when I fed Danny, and then Tommy and I had some tea. I fell asleep again at around five. When I woke up, the police were here."

A wailing noise came from outside the room and Agatha rose to her feet with a heretofore-undemonstrated alacrity. "Excuse me." She left the room.

Rowan tapped his foot, stood up, and walked over to the mantel. One of the photographs drew his attention.

Walter, embarrassed by the silence, turned to Tommy. "It's a lovely home."

"Ain't it? You can't buy good taste."

Rowan straightened an old photo of two little boys. The younger one was crying.

Tommy said, "That's Martin and me. See that teddy he's holding? That was my teddy. He knew if he took it from me, I'd start chopping onions. Sure enough, when the photographer told us to say cheese, Martin ripped it from my arms."

Rowan said, "I take it that you and your brother were very close."

"Well, I lived down in Mississippi for a while and we didn't see each other. I moved back a few months ago and we reconnected. Blood's forever." He pulled two stubs from his pocket. "We were supposed to go to the game today. It just didn't seem right for me to go without him."

Walter said, "Do you follow the Cubs?"

"Unfortunately, I do."

"Oh, I think they'll do quite well this year."

Tommy laughed wolfishly. "If every other team's train crashes and they all die in a fiery wreck, the Cubs might finish in second place. That's about the best we can hope for."

Walter said, "I'm optimistic. I think they have a chance to win it all."

"Spoken like a true Chicagoan."

Rowan's eyes slanted to the clock and he ran his tongue along a crack in his molar.

Walter leaned toward Tommy as if relaying a secret. "If I were the manager, I'd put Riggs Stephenson in the lineup every day. He's a genius with a bat."

"Riggs can hit, but he can't throw. I've got a better arm."

"He's the best hitter on the team. You've got to put him in the lineup. Keeping him on the bench is suicide."

One word from their conversation lit a fire in Rowan's brain.

*What are the chances?*

Tommy said, "Now their pitching is a different story."

Rowan shuffled his feet to the window. "Wait."

Walter knew this tone. "What is it, old man?"

"Have you noticed the names?" He snapped his fingers at Walter. "Williams, what are the strange names on the Bears?"

21

"You mean the Cubs."

"Whatever."

"Oh, yes. Ummm. Let's see, there's Hack, Gabby, Sheriff…"

Rowan slapped Tommy's arm as if they were friends. "Why do baseball players have such odd names?"

Tommy pushed both bushy eyebrows down. "I believe those are nicknames. I'm sure their mamas gave them proper biblical names when they were born."

Rowan nodded. "That is good thinking, Tommy. Although, Sheriff is a proper Scottish name and Riggs is an English name. Why, there is a company called 'Riggs Furniture' in New York." He shot Walter a look.

Walter said, "Yes, and Walter Riggs is a famous football coach. I'm not sure about Hack."

Tommy said, "Martin owned a company called Riggs, but it doesn't deal in furniture. And don't forget General Riggs, the war hero. I guess it's not so uncommon. Hey, we forgot the strangest name of all – Babe Ruth. I know he isn't on the Cubs, but that's got to be the name that takes the cake. It takes a lot of bee's nuts to go by Babe."

Rowan's smile turned smug again. "Yes, it does."

Agatha returned and sat on the sofa, rocking Danny in her arms.

Rowan returned to her side. "Mrs. Brent, I do not wish to take up much more of your time. There were two murders last winter that were eerily similar to the one of your husband. I believe we may be dealing with a maniac, someone with a compulsion to kill."

"Really? The police ruled out that idea. They said Martin must have had some connection to the man who killed him."

"They often bungle their investigations." Rowan craned his neck toward Tommy. "How long did they hold you for questioning?"

Tommy said, "The bastards had me in there for two whole days."

Rowan turned back to Agatha. "There you have it. A man who was in the room with you during the time of the murder was held overnight before being released. It is a scandalous waste of resources."

"It is rather alarming, I suppose."

Rowan clutched at his neck. "Mrs. Brent, I'm terribly sorry to bother you. My throat is quite dry. May I have some water?"

Agatha said, "Tommy, could you get Mr. Manory a glass of water?"

"Sure, sure." Tommy left the room.

Agatha looked down at her son. "I don't understand why someone would do such a thing if there was nothing to gain—"

Rowan pressed his hands against her cheeks and lifted her head up. He put his nose against her mouth and breathed in.

Walter recoiled in confusion. "Manory?"

When Rowan pulled back, Agatha didn't move. She tried to speak. "I... I..."

Rowan licked his lips. "Have you been eating garlic, Mrs. Brent?"

She let out a breathless word. "No."

"Funny that. Your breath reeks of garlic." He clutched her hands and lifted them up. "You have lovely nails, except for these lines." He ran a nicotine-stained finger over the white lines on her nails. "Have you always had them?"

Her head shook in a dazed circle. "No. They have appeared only recently."

"I see. I am going to ask you a few more questions, Mrs. Brent. We do not have much time. Please answer them quickly. How many clocks are in the house?"

"There are three, but—"

"But two of them are broken?"

"Yes."

"They have been broken for about three weeks?"

"Yes."

"On the day of your husband's murder, you say that you went to sleep at five o'clock?"

"Yes, I told you."

"Where did you drift off to sleep?"

"Here on the sofa with Danny."

"Uh-huh. What does Tommy do around the house?"

"Many things. He does the dishes and—"

"Does he make you tea?"

"Yes."

"Did he make the tea you drank before you went to sleep?"

"Yes."

Rowan put his hand on her knee. "Thank you, Mrs. Brent. Williams and I are going to take you away from here."

"Where are you taking me?"

"To the hospital."

"But why?"

"You are being poisoned, Mrs. Brent. You are being slowly poisoned with arsenic."

Tommy entered the living room with a glass of water. He set it on the coffee table. "Here you are, Mr. Manory, some old-fashioned double h zero."

Rowan stood up and returned to the mantel. He looked again at the photo of the Brent boys. "Williams, did you remember to set the clock in our office forward for the spring preservation of daylight?"

Walter put his notebook away. "I did it on the thirteenth." He moved to the doors and casually stood in front of them.

Rowan pointed to the clock. "Tommy, did you set this clock forward?"

"Yes, I believe I did. Fall back, spring forward."

"And did you set the clock forward a second time?"

Tommy did not answer.

"Nothing to say?" Rowan cocked his head. "No chitchat? No empty blather?" He grabbed the top of the clock and spun it around, displaying the winding mechanism and then began pacing around the room. "You are not the first man to manipulate a clock for the provision of an alibi, and I am sure you will not be the last. It is a very old trick. You see, on March the second in this year of our lord, you turned this clock back an hour. You rudely woke the baby up and ran to the living room. This is the room where Agatha brings Danny when she needs to calm him down. I can tell by how peaceful it is. You sat making small talk and sweating. At some point, you brought her tea laced with a sleeping agent. Perhaps it was Veronal; the details can be sorted out later. She fell asleep at five according to this clock, but we both know what the time really was. I do not even have to check the other two clocks to make sure you tampered with them. Do you know why?"

Tommy remained silent.

"It is because I am a superior judge of character."

Tommy patted the air with his hands. "Now, just hold up a minute. Before you get all heroic, you had better think this thing through, Mr. Manory. When I was being questioned, the cops had the same notion as you. You aren't that smart. There's no proof I did it. You need proof in this country."

"Oh, Tommy, you will make a fine corpse someday. You are already dead from the neck up. Some people just love to talk. Well, you may have talked yourself right into the electric chair. You see, I happen to know that your brother purchased the Riggs Tractor Company at four twenty on March the second. But how would you know that? The sale was completed just before his death. How could you know that? It would be impossible, unless you were in the office during the phone call." Rowan's face turned vindictive. "Did you enjoy choking the life out of him?"

Agatha's mouth crumpled.

Tommy turned white with anxiety. His body tensed.

Rowan said, "Now, here is what will happen next. Williams and I are going to take Mrs. Brent and Danny to the hospital. She can receive treatment for the trace amounts of arsenic you have been slipping into her drinks. If you develop a sudden onset of intelligence, you will turn yourself in. Perhaps a good lawyer can ensure you see the sunlight again."

Tommy Brent pulled out a gun and backed up. He swung it from Walter to Rowan. Finally, he settled on Rowan with a shaky hand. He swallowed. "Come on, Mr. Williams. Say something witty. Dazzle me."

Rowan took a deep breath. "This will not help you, Tommy. It will only make things worse." He walked a step closer to the gun.

Agatha summoned the strength to pull Danny tightly to her chest. The baby felt his mother's heartbeat quicken and began wailing anew. The sound grew more and more barbaric and uncontrolled, affecting the nervous systems of the four adults in the room.

Rowan took one more step. He desperately wanted a cigarette. "Let us think about a possible solution."

The exploding booms of the two bullets were followed by confused silence. Rowan mentally searched his body for the pain. There was none. He looked at Walter and saw him aghast. He turned around. The baby lay dead on Agatha's chest. Spattered blood covered the white sofa. Agatha's eyes were directed toward the detective. They hovered for a second and then the faint gleam inside them faded into nothing.

Tommy wore a ghastly sneer. His eyes became glossy. He shoved the gun in his own mouth and pulled the trigger.

Rowan's vision became blurry and his heart pounded. He heard Walter's voice echo in his head until everything went black.

# CHAPTER 2

# HOW VERY PECULIAR

The cigarette smoke flared against Rowan's cracked lips. He scuffed his shoes along the floor and pushed open the window. A stifling rush of July air shot against him like a blast from a furnace. Beads of sweat led trails down his temples and settled in the corners of his eyes.

Doctor Ling betrayed no emotion when he spoke. "Are you uncomfortable, Mr. Manory?"

"A bit. This office is as hot as Hades in the summer because of the bakery downstairs." He took one last drag off the sweat-soaked cigarette and then flicked it onto the street. "I will be fine."

"Are you ready to continue?"

Rowan pushed his cheek out with his tongue. Why wasn't Ling sweating? He was pudgy around the sides of his waistline and wore multiple layers.

"All hypnosis is self-hypnosis. Most people don't understand this fact. You can allow yourself to be hypnotized, but I cannot force you." Ling pressed his mustache against his upper lip. "Are you willing to allow it?"

Rowan nodded.

*I am desperate enough.*

"Close your eyes and breathe." Ling took deep noisy breaths to demonstrate. He inflected a purr at the end of every statement. "Good. Now, past your chest. Breathe into your knees."

"You want me to breathe into my knees?"

"Don't interpret everything in a literal sense. Breathe so deeply that the breath goes to your knees. I want you to imagine the room where it happened: the details of the furniture and the air and the people. Can you see?"

"Yes."

"Good. Don't forget to keep breathing. Tell me what you see."

Rowan told him everything he could remember about that horrible day in March: the curtains, the angels, Tommy's hair, and little Danny. He told Ling about the thrill of solving the case. Finally, he spoke about Agatha's eyes. He would never forget the sight of them.

"It was my job to protect her. I was so ecstatic to have solved the case that I did not think about the danger."

"What happens next?"

The sound of a backfiring car blasted from outside Rowan's office. His vision dimmed and mottled patches of black covered the image of Agatha and the baby.

Ling's voice began to echo. "You do not look so good, Manory. Is it happening now?"

The smell of the bakery vanished and was replaced by the horrible scent of copper. A paralyzing pain gripped Rowan's chest and the pounding of his heart battered his sense of hearing. He tried to speak, but the airless feeling inside his throat made it seem as if he could not produce any sound. Agatha's house vanished and Rowan found himself in a narrow darkened passage. The membranous walls pulsated closer and closer until they pressed against his body.

In the distance, Doctor Ling's voice bubbled as if it were submerged. "I think it is happening now, correct? Nod if this is true."

Rowan could not tell if his body was obeying his mind. He did his best to command a nod.

"Good. Detective, I want you to picture your heart. See your heart in your mind."

The diseased sack of red, bulbous flesh rattled after every beat as if it were about to explode in his chest. Blood leaked from a series of fissures.

"Now, picture black ink pouring all over your heart. It covers everything. Fill up the chamber with black ink."

Thick, black ooze drenched his imaginary organ until only the barest shape could be seen. He tried to nod again.

"Super. Now let it drain. The ink drains from your heart and all the pain and poison and infection are clinging to the ink as it separates. Can you see it, detective?"

Rowan managed to utter a breathless word. "Yes."

His heart appeared as a pristine pink.

"This is the last part. Imagine a spinning top."

"Huh?"

"It's the toy that children play with. Picture it on your heart. It spins clockwise. Put your finger on the top and stop it."

Rowan lifted his hand feebly.

"Not on your stomach, on your heart. Higher."

The detective visualized the top slowing and then coming to a halt under his fingertip.

"You're doing fabulous work. Spin it in the opposite direction."

Rowan's finger rotated over his chest. The top spun counterclockwise. As it picked up speed, the pressure lifted and his breath returned. Calm warmth emanated from his breast and spread through his limbs.

"Open your eyes."

Rowan tried to stand, but his legs wobbled. "What is wrong with me?"

"It's very simple. You have shell shock like a soldier after war."

"How do I cure it?"

"You don't cure it. You deal. Also, you are no longer a detective. You are officially retired."

"The treatment you gave me—"

"It wasn't treatment, Mr. Manory. It was a parlor trick. How you deal with your illness is up to you. I'm simply your guide, your Sherpa, your cicerone—"

"I know what guide means."

"To stop being a prisoner of the past, one must face the past and master it. That is the goal. In the meantime you suffer. Shall we meet again next week?"

Rowan collapsed into his chair with limp limbs. "I will think it over."

"I'll send you the bill. Good day."

Ling left without closing the office door. Rowan could hear him speaking with Walter in the hall. He tugged at his collar and it bent with sweat.

Walter entered as if he was visiting his grandmother. "I brought you a sardolive." He shoved aside the pile of old newspapers on Rowan's desk and swept scattered ash into the trashcan. "They make them downstairs."

"You know I have no appetite." Rowan sat up and pulled off his tie. "This weather is unbearable."

"Yeah, it's a corker. You have to start eating, though." Walter put a brown paper bag on the desk and laid the sandwich on top. Next to it, he laid down a stack of envelopes. "Come now. You have to try."

Rowan lifted the top slice of rye bread. A pile of sardines and diced olives lay bathed in creamy egg yolk. His stomach gurgled into a knot and his unshaven face began to itch.

"It's very tasty," said Walter.

"I will take you at your word." Rowan rolled his head from shoulder to shoulder, cracked his knuckles, and grabbed the envelopes. He read the return addresses of the first three and threw them into the trash. He stopped at the fourth.

Walter asked, "Someone we know?"

"The sender is Robert Lasciva from Vicksburg, Mississippi." Rowan laid a paper on his desk and spread tobacco over it. He licked one end and, with a single motion, twirled it into a cigarette. "Lasciva. Lasciva. I have heard the name but cannot recall where." He tossed it to Walter. "Open it."

"How do you know it's not more hate mail?"

"There are no temper strokes. When a writer is angry, he begins the first letters from underneath the baseline."

"It could be passive aggressive. Are there condescension strokes?"

"Very funny. Read me the letter."

"Are you going to eat the sandwich I bought you?"

"Williams!"

Walter ripped open the envelope and read aloud.


*Dear Mr. Rowan Manory,*

*My name is Robert Lasciva and I am in need of your services. I'll cut right to the chase. Recently, I received a death threat in the mail. This threat promises that I will be murdered during the weekend of my fifty-fifth birthday and that the murderer will be a guest at my party. My birthday is on the seventh of August and I'm having a small, tight-knit celebration lasting from the fifth to the eighth.*

*I'd like to hire you to attend the party and mingle with the guests to see if any of them might be planning something dramatic. I would not* inform anyone, even my bodyguard, that you are a detective. I live in Vicksburg, Mississippi, which is far from your base of operations in Chicago. Because of this, I would be willing to pay you the sum of three thousand dollars for the weekend. This figure is guaranteed regardless of outcome and will be paid in cash on the eighth. I'm sure your license doesn't exceed the Illinois border, but the government needn't know anything. Uncle Sam has more important things to worry about.

If you accept, there will be a Model T waiting for you at the local Saunders in the town of Olive Branch. It's in the north of Mississippi. You can use it to drive the rest of your journey to Vicksburg. We are currently in the middle of a particularly nasty flood. My estate is located high upon a ridge between the Bayou Pierre Mounds and Fort Hill. There is a road about 400 feet above the valley that will get you here safely. I have included a map showing the route.

There are only three guests I have invited to the party along with my staff and business associates. The list:

Bernice Lasciva - my aunt

Charles Lasciva - my nephew

Margaret Lasciva - his wife

Jack Tellum - my bodyguard

Paul Daniels - my lawyer

Ruth Martice - my secretary

Willie Aikes - my butler and driver

I can't imagine any of these people wanting to do me any harm but I'd like you here to see if I am mistaken. Please let me know your decision post haste.


Regards,

Robert Lasciva


Rowan stared past the wall. An inch-long piece of ash hung from his cigarette. "How very peculiar."

Walter gawped. "Holy…" He mouthed the second word. "Three thousand rubes. That's—" He looked at Rowan. "Of course, you're not taking the job?"

"No, I... No." Rowan folded the letter and pocketed it. "You are quite correct, my friend. Even my despondency cannot compel me to take such an extreme risk. The name is familiar, though."

"I will say this." Walter took a bite of the sardolive and wiped a bit of yolk off his mouth. "Going to a new city might not be a bad idea. I don't mean setting up the same operation. We could retire from murder and focus on infidelity. California's nice this time of year. In fact, it's nice every time of the year."

Rowan stared daggers. "I do not care what the Chinese quack says."

"Manory, we haven't had a client in four months."

"One bit of good press and that problem will be solved. The public has no collective memory."

"What about your heart?"

Rowan mimicked Ling's voice. "I deal."

"Do you mind if I ask you something?"

"Stop tagging your questions. Just ask."

"Does your despondency compel you to come with me to the pharmacist?"

An hour later, the detectives walked into the Brown Bear and sidled up to the bar.

Before prohibition, the Brown Bear had been a popular destination for casual and chronic drinker alike. Like many bars in Chicago, its survival during the dry hysteria depended on ingenuity. Those with bribable doctors could procure a ten-ounce weekly prescription. Alcohol became a cure-all. Studies were commissioned to prove that vodka cured syphilis, gin was good for arthritis, and beer stopped the flu dead in its tracks.

Dave Bowen, the bartender, polished two glasses and slid them over the red wood. He leaned on the copper beer pump. "What can I get you?"

Walter pulled out his wallet. "I'll have a whiskey and a brandy for my friend."

"Let's see 'em."

Walter and Rowan took out their prescriptions and placed them on the bar.

Dave slid a pen from his breast pocket and wrote down the ounces and the date. He looked at Walter. "How are the migraines?"

"They get better with every visit."

Dave turned to Rowan. His face scrunched up. "Gout? Is that French?"

"Yes, I believe so."

The bartender sighed. "All right boys, let's see. Mr. Williams, you have eight ounces left. Mr. Manory, you only have two. Looks like you'll have to go back to the doctor."

"I will return with a more romantic illness."

Dave poured the drinks.

Walter said, "Does anyone ever come in with alcoholism?"

"Funnily enough, no. You see that guy at the end of the bar." He motioned toward a burly man with bushy sideburns. "His doc gave him scurvy. I had a bit of fun and told him I had to put a lime in all of his drinks. He nearly shit himself."

They took their glasses and walked to their usual table, next to the eponymous stuffed brown bear in the center of the room.

They patted the leg for good luck.

Walter leaned back in his chair and began to pour out his thoughts, as was his custom. Rowan was quiet. He seemed distracted.

"You have to be flexible, Manory. We can do anything we want. There's no reason to stay. Chicago must be the most miserable city in the world. The weather is deadly and the people are even worse. There's no beauty here."

*Where have I heard the name?*

Walter twirled his finger round the rim of his glass. "Maybe there's a little beauty. You know who I can't get out of my head?"

*Robert Lasciva.*

"Miss Amanda Green. I think about her at least once a week. Isn't

40

it strange how that happens? One little moment gets into your head and then it comes back again and again. I have an obsession. That's what I've got."

*Was he from the Cockrill case?*

"I'm not sure you noticed, but when you were questioning her, she kept looking at me. She didn't say anything, but her eyes said volumes. It's like you always tell me, the eyes say much more than the mouth."

*No, it was a different case. Which one?*

"Do you think she was vamping with me? I think she was. I'm a single man who is young, not terribly young, but younger than you. You're not old, but in contrast… You know what I mean."

*Your brain is broken. You never forgot anything before…before… You cannot even say his name.*

"I know she's in prison, but she could be out in five to ten. Women get far more lenient treatment from the penal system. She'll be in her mid-thirties, perhaps a bit haggard, but still easy on the eyes."

*Before Tommy Brent. You never forgot anything before Tommy Brent.*

"There's the nasty business about murdering her husband, but if she was with the right man, I think she could be passionately rehabilitated." Walter swirled his glass. "I hope she doesn't get attacked in prison."

*The name Lasciva is from a case. I know that. But which one?*

"Are there knife fights in female prisons?"

41

Rowan came out of his stupor. "What?"

"Shanks or razors? Do female inmates cut each other like men do?"

"What in the hell are you talking about?"

"Do you think Amanda Green could be attacked in prison with a sharp object? I'm specifically thinking about her face."

"How would I know?"

"Your mother was a member of the police force and she dealt with female prisoners. Did she tell you anything about the prisons?"

"My mother?"

It came to him all at once. The creases on his forehead and temples smoothed out. A look of astonishment flashed onto his face.

Walter panicked. "Is this another episode? Shall I fetch Dr. Ling?"

"Williams!"

"What is it, old man?"

Rowan shoved his hand inside his pocket and ripped out the letter. He slammed it on the table and his index finger tapped it maniacally. "Robert Lasciva."

"You know him."

"I have never met the man, but he has a certain reputation. Do we have contacts in Mississippi?"

"Yeah, I can call a few people."

"Find out everything you can. I want to know what he is doing there and with whom he is doing it. Do it now. Do not delay." Rowan slammed back his brandy and stood up.

"Where are you going?"

"I must talk to my last friend on the police force."

# CHAPTER 3

# DIGGING UP THE DOROTHY ROBERTS CASE

"Extraordinary." Rowan flipped the police report back and forth in an attempt to make sense of it all. His head came up. He simply repeated, "Extraordinary."

"Yeah, it's a dilly of a quagmire." Inspector Grady glanced over his shoulder at the café door. He sat with his side leaning on the back of the chair. "Ten more minutes, champ. Then I have to go."

"Robert Lasciva and Jack Tellum were seen leaving the apartment building by multiple witnesses. Irene Roberts had bitten Tellum and the teeth marks were verified. When they were picked up that evening, both Lasciva and Tellum had her blood on their goddamned shirts. The mother, Dorothy Roberts, ended up dead on the street below. And yet, no charges were ever filed. The newspapers never even mentioned that Irene was in the room. What am I missing?"

Grady glowered. "You're not that dense."

"Hold my hand, please."

The waitress brought two lemonades to the table. Grady waited for her to leave and leaned his head toward Rowan. "We were told the case was finished. I wasn't in charge and there were plenty of other things to work on. Your mother, God rest her soul, she made the biggest stink about it. Look what happened. Ellen was demoted."

"What was Lasciva's hold on the department?"

"He had a lawyer. What was his name?" Grady looked around at the empty tables for help.

Rowan pulled the letter from his pocket. "Paul Daniels?"

He snapped his fingers. "That's it. Daniels. He was a real squirrelly fella, never kept still. He talked like a swish, but from what I hear it wasn't the case. Anyway, he had the superintendent's ear. You didn't hear it from me, but he also had a direct line to his bank account."

Rowan kept his gaze on Grady.

"Don't be a boy scout; you know how things work. Besides, Irene Roberts never fingered Lasciva or Tellum for the crime. It's hard to put somebody away if the only witness won't talk. As far as I know, she never told anybody what happened in that room. She just kept saying that nursery rhyme, over and over again. Her mental state was described as catatonic." He pointed to the report. "It was decided that we shouldn't reveal anything to the public about her. Woman kills herself. Two men questioned and released. It's a lot cleaner."

"If he had nothing to fear from the police, why did Lasciva leave Chicago?"

Grady cackled and coughed out his words. "That was your mother's doing."

Rowan shook his head dumbly.

"Ellen Manory was the sweetest thing I ever met, but you didn't want to get on her bad side. She told them."

"She told whom?"

"She told *them*. She told Mont Tennes, Mickey Finn, she told every gang leader in town, sent them all anonymous letters with all the perversity intact."

Rowan pictured his mother's sweet comforting visage.

Grady gulped half his lemonade. "It's twisted when you think about it. Last week a bomb went off in Dukes, the speakeasy on Wabash. One of Capone's guys planted a bomb in a little boy's schoolbag and told him to go in there and wait ten minutes. These bastards will kill a child without a moment's hesitation. But, if you do what Lasciva did to Irene Roberts…" He shook his head. "It's some kind of morality, I suppose."

"So, Dorothy Roberts commits suicide and Irene Roberts is assaulted and her attackers are never found. That is the end of it?"

47

"That's the long and the short of it, champ. Life goes on."

"What happened to Irene?"

Grady took a long breath. "Are you sure you want to be doing this. You don't look well."

"I have had a bad year."

"There are rumors about you, you know? They say you've gone Rorschach after what happened to the Brent lady. Maybe it's time to retire. My guess is you aren't sleeping. It happens when you get a bit of blood on your hands."

Rowan cast a sour glance.

"Go home, Manory. Find some little girl's lost kitten. The Roberts case has been buried for twenty years; don't go digging it up. All that's left is the rotting of the bodies."

Rowan rolled a cigarette with unearthly calm. "You can tell me what happened to Irene or I can run around town all day and find out. I would hope your friendship with my mother would compel you to assist me."

Grady's face turned hard.

Rowan lit his cigarette and pointed the butt end at Grady. "What happened to Irene?"

Grady's voice rose. "This is the last time I help you. In fact, this is the last time we speak. If I get caught discussing police business with a private citizen, I'll be suspended or worse." He snatched Rowan's cigarette and stuck it in his own mouth. "After she recovered, Irene Roberts was adopted by a German family. They were friends of Dorothy. The social office thought it would be a good place for her. From what I understand, it was."

Rowan took out a pencil and notebook. "What are their names?"

"Gunther and Alice Schmidt. They lived near Fullerton and Damon. I can't remember the exact address. Nice folks. Your mother checked in on them from time to time to see how Irene was doing. She was just like you, couldn't let anything go."

Rowan held the pencil to the notebook. "Is Irene still living there?"

He sighed. "This story doesn't have a happy ending."

"None do."

"It musta been about 1914. Yeah, I'm sure, 'cause it was the year I met my wife. That summer, four kids went missing from the neighborhood."

"One of them was Irene."

"That's right, one of them was Irene. We had a lot of people on the case. Ellen interviewed the mothers. You don't remember this?"

"My mother never discussed her work with me."

"Good policy. We caught the guy who did it. Gale was his name, Frank Gale. We found three of the bodies buried in his cellar. It was a notorious case. The library can give you all the details."

"Four children went missing and you found three bodies. Why do I already know the name of the missing body?"

Grady looked at his shoes. "Gale confessed to three murders, but he claimed he didn't kill Irene. For a week, he kept up his story. Finally, he confessed. He was hanged the following spring."

The pencil dropped. "This is unbearable."

"Manory—"

"After a week of beatings, I would confess to the murder of Irene Roberts."

"The case is closed."

"It took him a week to confess? He had no problem copping to the other murders though, did he? With Irene Roberts, he suddenly gets skittish?"

"They call it abnormal behavior for a good reason."

"What happened to the body?"

"He said he threw it in the river. It was never found."

Rowan buried his hands in his hair and tugged. "Are the Schmidts still alive?"

"I know the husband died. The wife, Alice, was in her sixties when Dorothy committed suicide. I don't know if she's still kicking." Grady finished his lemonade. "Your ten minutes are up, champ. Take my advice, leave it alone."

Rowan pointed to the file. "May I keep this?"

Grady made a raspberry sound with his mouth, took the manila envelope, and left without saying goodbye.


Alice Schmidt looked at Rowan through fat glasses suspended over the bridge of her nose. Her left eye was hazel and the right one clouded over by a pearly storm. Her body, ravaged by physiologic tremor, shook in violent, arrhythmic bursts. She spoke with half of her mouth paralyzed.

"Do you want tea?" she asked.

"That would be lovely," said Rowan.

"I have no tea."

"It is of no importance."

"I have water."

"That would be fine."

"It is brown."

Rowan placed his hands flat on the table and watched her walk in stuttered half steps to the sink. The barren kitchen showed no signs of food. Cracks indented the walls and mold covered the better part of the ceiling. Each drawer of the cabinet lay crooked in its housing and Rowan fought off the urge to straighten them.

Alice turned on the tap. The water pipes groaned to life. "I don't know why you want to talk to me. Everything has been decided, no?"

"Cases are reopened all the time, Frau Schmidt. Circumstances change; new evidence is brought to light."

"Did the circumstances change?"

He waited for her to bring the water to the table. "Not exactly, but let me simply say I am not satisfied. Thank you."

She leaned her backside over the chair and held it suspended until gravity pulled it down. "You are police?"

"No. I am a private investigator."

"And who is paying you to investigate?"

"There is no client. I am here on my own."

"A man who does not do a thing for money must do it for some other reason."

He set the glass to the side. "Frau Schmidt, do you not recognize my name?"

She stared blankly.

"My name is Manory. My mother was Ellen Manory. She was a policewoman. She worked on the Dorothy Roberts case. I know she spoke with you quite a few times."

"I remember Ellen. You are her son?"

"Yes."

Alice squinted her eye. "You look nothing like her. Usually boys look like their mother."

He scratched his stubble. "I am having a bad year."

"Where is Ellen now?"

"She passed away."

"But she was so young. How?"

Rowan tilted his head. "What?"

"Your mother, how did she die?"

"How did she die?" He thought for a moment. "Natural causes."

The corner of Alice's lip curled. "Death is natural, isn't it?"

"Frau Schmidt, when Irene Roberts came to live with you—"

"Do you have any children?"

Rowan bit his lip. "No."

"Why not?"

He laughed. "That is a very long conversation."

Her voice turned commanding at the first opportunity. "I do not want anything from you, Herr Manory. It seems you want something from me, though. Why don't you have any children?"

"My profession is not conducive to family life. It can be dangerous, and the time invested in each case is restrictive."

"Klappspaten."

Rowan did not speak German, but he understood an insult when he heard one.

Alice said, "You will see. Everyone you know will die and then you will be alone with no one to talk to. You will wonder if any of your life really happened, if anything you remember was real. That is why people have children. My husband and I could not have any of our own, but we had Irene, for a time."

Rowan made a steeple of his fingers. "In three weeks I will go to see Robert Lasciva at his home in Mississippi. I think you know this man. You know what he did and you know that of which he is capable."

For a moment, her body ceased its movement. She almost smiled. "Are you a good detective, Herr Manory?"

He answered without hesitation. "I am the best detective I know."

"Die besten schwimmer ertrinken."

Rowan questioned her with his eyebrows.

"The best swimmers drown."

"Please, Frau Schmidt."

She sighed and leaned back on the chair. The creak echoed. "Dorothy's husband died. He was a foolish man, but he worked. A man who works is not altogether bad. Gunther and I offered to help with Irene. We loved Irene. She was so little. Mäuschen."

"Mowshen?"

"Little mouse. Irene had teeth like a mouse." She lifted two wrinkled fingers and pointed them down in front of her mouth. "Dorothy got a job as an operator and Irene stayed with us during the day. We were like her grandparents."

"When did Dorothy start seeing Lasciva?"

"I don't know. She never told me about it."

"Did she know who he was?"

"Everyone in the neighborhood knew who he was. I should say everyone suspected. Someone would turn up dead and his name would be mentioned. There were rumors."

"Why would someone like Dorothy…" He considered his phrasing.

Alice answered the unfinished question. "She was lonely, Herr Manory. Do you ever get lonely?"

He nodded. "You saw her on the night she died."

"Dorothy was walking but it didn't seem like she was going anywhere. How do you say this?"

"Aimlessly."

"Yes, without aim. I invited her in, but she said she had to get home to Irene."

"When Dorothy committed suicide—"

"She did not do any suicide."

"You think she was pushed out of the window?"

"It was not suicide. She was driven to it."

Rowan froze and lost his train of thought. He heard his heartbeat. "When Irene came to live with you, did she ever say what happened that night?"

Alice shook her head. "Never. Gunther said it was the mind's natural reaction to such a traumatic experience. It will erase that which is bad to remember. Irene had nightmares. I think that is when she remembered."

The faint sound of playing children came through the window.

Rowan dropped his head to meet her gaze. "Seven years later, she was murdered."

"She walked home from the school the same way every day. It was so unusual."

"What?"

"I knew she wouldn't come home that day. I was waiting for her to walk down the street and I knew something was wrong. My gut always knows the truth."

"She was murdered by a man named Gale."

"That is what they said."

"Gale kidnapped and killed two girls…" Rowan checked his notebook, "…aged five and six, and a boy, aged six. He disemboweled the first girl and buried her in his cellar. The second victim was also disemboweled and buried next to the first girl and the corpses were made to hold hands. This was repeated with the third. Then, inexplicably, he murdered Irene at the age of fourteen. He unceremoniously dumped her body in the Chicago River. It is quite odd, this sudden change in modus operandi."

"Isn't it?" Alice's arms began to rattle the table and she removed them. "Gale had family in Chicago. He had a sister and two nephews. After he confessed to killing Irene, I heard they moved to New York. They live in a very nice house."

"Is that true?"

"It's only what I heard."

"It is almost as if his sister received money after he confessed."

She nodded.

"It is almost as if someone else killed Irene and paid off Gale's family on the condition that he confessed to the murder."

"Yes, Herr Manory."

His eyes looked at nothing as the gears turned in his head. "Thank you, Frau Schmidt. I must go."

He made it halfway to the door.

"Herr Manory!" She pushed her forearms against the table in an effort to stand. The shift in weight caused her to collapse on the floor.

Rowan ran to her and put his hand on the side of her face. The wrinkled skin was rubbery to the touch.

She struggled to communicate through huffed breath. Her words hissed past her tongue. "I want to know."

"Know what?"

"I want to know what happened to my mäuschen. Every detail."

"Frau Schmidt—"

She grabbed his wide lapel. "Promise me, Herr Manory. Promise me, you will find out and you will tell me. Not knowing is agony. I have nothing, you can see it." Her eye darted round the kitchen. "You will come back and you will tell me how she died. I need to know."

"I will tell you everything I find out."

Her face grew sullen.

"I am telling you the truth, I swear it."

"You say it now, but I am afraid you will disappoint me."

Rowan hesitated. He grimaced. "Frau Schmidt?"

"Yes?"

"My mother's death. There was nothing natural about it."


Rowan sliced the steak into identical ragged red cubes. His fork pierced four of them in quick succession. He was still chewing when Walter sat at the table.

"You shaved."

Rowan grunted.

"I'll wait until you've finished." Walter set his notebook on the table.

Rowan held up his hand and made a circular motion in the air.

Walter said, "Hello, Williams. It's so nice to see you. I've been so busy lately. I just wanted to let you know how much I appreciate all your hard work."

Rowan chewed faster and swallowed. "Hello, Williams. It is so nice to see you. I have been so busy lately. I just wanted to let you know how much I appreciate all your hard work. Now, out with it."

Walter grinned. "Lasciva is a very interesting character. He arrived in Mississippi in 1908 with Tellum and Daniels in tow. They ran a few nightclubs. There were rumors about where he came from but nobody knew for sure. It seems he lived a pretty quiet life."

"Until?"

"Until Prohibition. Mississippi is known as the wettest dry state. It has one of the biggest bootlegging operations in the country. He ships quite a bit of booze out of there and the majority of it ends up in Chicago with his old friends. Everyone in Mississippi seems to know about it, but the law doesn't touch him."

"Some things never change."

"There's something I want to ask you."

"Yes?"

"Something I couldn't find out."

"Just ask."

"Why did he leave Chicago in the first place?"

Rowan shrugged. He pointed at the notes with his steak knife.

"What about his house?"

"It's not a house, it's a goddamned mansion. It's famous."

"Very fancy?"

"No, I mean it's *famous*. Walter Anderson photographed it in 1925. He's the guy who photographs the White House every year. The pictures of Lasciva Manor are in the art museum in Jackson."

"It seems he no longer has any interest in keeping a low profile."

"I called the curator and he read me the description. Listen to this. 'Sitting on an anomalous plateau on the ridge, the manor and its surrounding area have been meticulously furbished to suit its owner's taste. The forest was carved out and the home was built over a period of three years. Willow trees have been transplanted into the thin soil and now adorn the grounds of the estate. A garden of wild zinnias sits behind the house and eventually morphs into the circumambient forest.' There's only one road that leads up to the place."

Rowan pulled out the letter. "And what of the other guests?"

"The butler's worked there for a few years and the secretary has only started recently. Nobody that I talked to knows anything about the

60

relatives."

"Anything else?"

"Lasciva wasn't kidding about the flood."

"Yes, I have seen the photographs."

"Apparently his home is in a good spot. The town below is covered in water."

Rowan wiped his mouth. "Nice work, Williams."

Walter waited for only a moment. "You're taking the case, aren't you?"

"I am taking the case."

"I knew it. There's never a dull moment, I suppose. When do we leave?"

"I will leave. You must stay here."

"Come again?"

"I must work alone, Williams. Everything I have learned tells me it will be dangerous. I cannot risk being responsible for you."

"That's funny because you're the one with the heart condition."

"Williams—"

"You can barely make it out of bed."

"I feel much better."

"What happens when you black out? Huh?"

"Listen to me—"

"No, no, no, I always listen to you, Manory. There are two ways this will pan out. The first is that we go together. The second is that we go separately. Knowing how you drive, I'll beat you there by three days and solve the case myself. You decide."

Rowan rested his head on his palm. "I cannot be responsible for your safety."

"That's right. I'm responsible for yours. Can I ask you something?"

"Just ask."

"If this is such a dangerous case, why are you taking it?"

He tapped his fork on the plate. "To stop being a prisoner of the past, one must face the past and master it."

# CHAPTER 4

# THE GREAT MISSISSIPPI FLOOD

Far above the flood, the Model T crept along the ridge. The town of Vicksburg had seen nothing but rain since the onset of spring and now twenty-five feet of water covered any signs of civilization. Here and there a roof or a tree peeked above the rampaging surface and occasionally objects would violently bob before being submerged again. The deluge had unearthed the contents of Beulah Cemetery and forced the coffins to travel through the town like some unholy pastiche of a funeral procession. No one knew if the worst had already happened. The constant cloudbursts suggested this was simply the way things were now. The carnage was visible through the rain-spattered window of the car as the detectives made their way to a most bizarre birthday party.

"Eyes forward, Williams," Rowan said.

Walter ignored his boss and continued shifting his eyes from the road to the valley below and then back again. "Have you ever seen anything like this, Manory? It's positively biblical."

Like so many towns along the Mississippi River, Vicksburg was no more. Most of the residents had fled months earlier. Those foolish enough to stay behind had perished, their bodies to be found three or four towns over. The final numbers of death and destruction had yet to be determined, but it was already the worst natural disaster in the history of the United States.

"Williams, you should concentrate on the driving of the car. If we die it will be impossible to collect our three thousand dollars."

Walter checked the speedometer. "Applesauce. We're going five miles per hour."

As if excited by the raging water, the wind gusted and shook the frame of the Model T. Rowan stamped his feet and tried to slow his breathing. The violent closing of valves echoed in his eardrums, threatening to take him out of reality.

The detective rolled a cigarette and placed it at the usual wild angle in the corner of his mouth. With the strike of the third match he finally inhaled balm for his lungs.

*You must focus on the case in front of you and not the one behind. Why did Lasciva hire me? He could have easily found a local detective. Why not simply cancel the party?*

Walter began tapping the steering wheel to the tune of 'Ain't She Sweet'.

Rowan reached over and grabbed his hand. "If you are going to start singing, let me out and I can walk the rest of the way."

"Manory?"

"What is it, Williams?"

"There is something I've long wondered about you."

"I detest your incessant tagging of inquiry. If you have a question to ask me, you should simply ask me and be done with it. If I want to know the time, I say, 'Williams, what is the time?' I do not say, 'Williams, I was wondering if you would not mind telling me something, something that has been on my mind.'"

"Usually, you are unflappable, the coolest customer."

"I appreciate the compliment but I still await the question."

"I've seen you deal with the most barbarous scum society can produce without a hint of sweat on your forehead. But all you have to do is sit in a car with some bad weather and you're inconsolable."

Rowan nodded. "This is very simple. I cannot reason with an automobile and I cannot outwit the weather. I am in my element when I am in control." He peered into the valley. A cow's carcass was lodged in the branches of a tree. "I fear there is no control in this situation."

"We've been driving all day, but we haven't discussed much about the case."

"I am still pondering it. When I reach a conclusion you will be the second to know."

"Do you think one of the guests has actually planned a murder?"

"We shall see."

"Surely you have a guess."

"What a careless statement. A good detective does not extrapolate feelings or guesses without evidence. I will know when I have read the threat for myself and profiled the partygoers. Until that point, my mind is open to any possibility. Ten o'clock, two o'clock, Williams."

Walter sighed and adjusted his hands on the steering wheel. The first rule about working with Rowan Manory was that Rowan Manory was always right. "Now that we're on our way, could you tell me what Lasciva did that was so bad?"

Silence.

"His girlfriend threw herself out the window. He didn't really do anything, did he?"

Rowan finally spoke. "The Roberts case was my mother's first on the police force. The city of Chicago only started hiring women for the sole purpose of interviewing women. Whether it is a suspect, victim, or witness, women feel more comfortable talking to women police officers. It is natural. My mother's function in the investigation was to interview the witness."

"I didn't know there was a witness."

"The daughter was in the room when the mother went through the window, a seven-year-old named Irene."

Lightning struck the valley and electricity spread in all directions on the water's surface.

"What did Irene tell the police?"

"Unfortunately, the girl said nothing of any consequence. According to the report, she was traumatized and just kept repeating a nursery rhyme."

Walter shifted in his seat and slowly maneuvered a bend in the road. "Perhaps the rhyme was some kind of clue."

Rowan shook his head. "I think not. Most likely it was something Dorothy Roberts had read to her before she slept. It was the one about the church bells."

"Church bells? How does it go?"

Rowan hummed and sang the rhyme.

*Orange and lemons*

*Say the bells of St. Clements*

*You owe me five farthings*

*Say the bells of St. Martins*

"It goes on and on like that. There are other church bells and then comes the final part."

*Here comes a candle*

*To light you to bed*

*Here comes a chopper*

*To chop off your head*

*Chip chop, chip chop*

*The last man's dead*

Walter chuckled. "Children's rhymes can be so incredibly dark. Do you recall the one about the corpse in the well that drags down any child foolish enough to play near it? I still find myself avoiding wells."

Rowan cleared his throat and turned conspiratorially to Walter. "Williams, the newspapers ran the story that Dorothy Roberts was found dead outside her apartment, a victim of suicide. Other details were left out. Keep your eyes on the road. It was never revealed to the public that the daughter had been raped, stabbed, and left for dead inside Roberts's bedroom. It was a miracle the girl survived."

"Jesus Christ." Walter took a moment for this grim revelation to sit in his mind. "Lasciva did it?"

"He was the primary suspect."

"Your mother thought he did it?"

He nodded.

The single wiper futilely battled the onslaught of rain as Walter pieced together all that he had heard until he came to a realization. He applied the brake and brought the car to a halt in the middle of the chaos. "Manory, what are we doing?"

"We are being paid to investigate a death threat, of course."

"So, we are working for a... We are working for the worst possible member of society."

"That is one way of putting it."

"This is the kind of person we investigate. This is not the kind of person we take on as a client. If someone killed Robert Lasciva, it would be no great loss to the world. We can't go through with this, Rowan."

"Do you not believe in innocent before proven guilty?"

"There's a finite point when that concept is no longer useful. Don't you believe in justice?"

Rowan stared Walter down. He grimaced. "No. I believe in the law."

"Technically, bootlegging is against the law."

Rowan jabbed his cigarette into the ashtray. "Let us not fool ourselves, my friend. One reason for taking this case is that our firm is in trouble. My incompetence during the Tommy Brent case—"

"Boss, you mustn't continue to blame yourself."

"My utter incompetence has caused irreparable harm and as a result, we have been on holiday for five months. We need the business." Rowan rolled another cigarette and absently twisted the butt end. "However, there is another reason. Irene Roberts was taken in by friends of the family, an old German couple. I paid a visit to the wife. Thirteen years ago Irene Roberts was murdered." He struggled to articulate his next thought. It was as if he could not bear the existence of his fear. Often, in lieu of these premonitions, Rowan would offer something generic to replace the conclusion his mind leaned toward. "There are some questions I have and I feel the answers are high on this ridge."

The detectives sat quietly.

Walter finally spoke. "I think I understand. We're being paid to investigate a death threat, but we're taking the case for another reason entirely."

"That is another way of putting it."

Rowan's vision shifted to the distance. Another flash of lightning temporarily illuminated the treetops. A large network of cylindrical barrels was suspended high in the tallest trees by ropes. The moonshine operation in Vicksburg had thwarted the weather and moved above the flood. This creative solution delighted him.

*And so, man becomes a monkey. Surely this is devolution at its most poetic.*

"Okay, Manory. I think it's a horrible idea, but I'm on board. Why didn't you tell me all of this before we left?"

"You would have tried harder to stop me from coming. Remember, my friend, I asked you to stay in Chicago. You refused. If you do not take my advice, you cannot complain."

"If I don't go with you then no one will have any fun."

"That is an excellent point that I have duly noted. Now drive, Williams. No more stopping. We are too late for the dinner, but perhaps we are not too late for the murder."

# CHAPTER 5

## GUESTS

Jack Tellum's mind blanked and his narration came to a halt. A hint of inner fury appeared. "Will you stop prancing around, Paulie? You're like a fly in an outhouse."

Paul Daniels stubbed out his seventh consecutive cigarette and promptly lit his eighth. Covered by a double-breasted white suit, the lawyer's slight, wispy frame ambulated back and forth along the library's wall of books as if looking for an exit. He bowed to Charles and Margaret. "My apologies. I didn't mean to interrupt such a fascinating tale. And it was just getting good too. Any minute now, we'll arrive at the thrilling denouement. Jack's going to wrap the whole thing up with a great big bow. Aren't you, Jack? The suspense is killing me." He sat on the only empty sofa and crossed his legs. The cigarette dangled from his index and middle fingers with the lit end precariously close to the armrest. "Please, continue."

Charles and Margaret Lasciva, ensconced on the library's center sofa, did not pay Daniels any mind. Their attention rested solely on the squat mass of flesh that was Jack Tellum. Robert Lasciva's nephew identified Tellum as the most dangerous thing in the room and suspected him capable of committing sudden acts of unprovoked violence. Charles envisioned elaborate scenarios where Tellum would turn on him with rage. His imaginative thoughts concluded with his death at the hands of the brute each and every time.

Tellum patted down his sweaty skull with a handkerchief. "One day you'll go too far, Paulie. One day it'll be too much sauce." He turned his head and upper torso to Margaret. "Yeah, well, where was I?"

Margaret held an exceedingly labored smile. "The crowbar?"

"That's right." He drank from his flask. "The crowbar is on the table and I'm two seconds from using it. Jerry says to me – and the whole time he's sticking out his chest like a dog trying to get some – so, he says, 'I'm taking the gin today and it's gonna be for the same price.' I couldn't believe it."

Margaret gently elbowed her husband in the ribs.

"Very presumptuous," said Charles, displaying a ghost of a grin.

"Yeah, well, you Brits say 'presumptuous' but I'd say the guy was begging for a closed casket at his funeral. That's when Paulie steps in to teach me about diplomacy. Paulie, weighing all of a buck twenty—"

"A buck sixty," Daniels corrected him with a slight lisp in his voice.

"Yeah well, big bad Paulie steps in and looks this pill dead in the eyes. He goes, 'Perhaps I might be able to elucidate the scenario' or some such nonsense. And he does. He explains to the guy what it would mean to his future business prospects and what would happen to his family. The man abided."

"And you didn't have to beat him to death with the crowbar," said Daniels.

"Yeah, well, that's why I love you, Paulie." A tingling sensation caused Tellum's head to momentarily feel weightless. He bit the skin of his bottom lip. "Brother is it hot."

Daniels pointed his cigarette at Charles. "Wasn't that a good story? Aren't you glad you stayed around until the end?"

Charles tightened his grip on Margaret's hand. "It sounds like everything worked itself out." He stammered for a few seconds and then looked to his wife.

Margaret cleared her throat. "Temperance is such a childish idea. One need only read an American newspaper to realize how terribly ineffective the whole thing is. There is the occasional talk of it in England, mostly from fundamentalist types. Cooler heads always prevail. Of course, we have a much longer history. They say the States haven't had the time to learn these kinds of lessons. What is your opinion on the matter, Mr. Daniels?"

Paul Daniels held his cigarette inches from his mouth for a few seconds. "And I thought *we* were boring. Jesus Christ."

Tellum snapped his fingers. "Be nice, Paulie."

Daniels hopped off the sofa and looked out the window. He checked his pocket watch. "Where is Mr. Manory?"

"This man we're waiting on, he's a friend of Uncle Robert?" asked Charles.

"He's Bob's best friend. They haven't seen each other for a long time," said Tellum. "A long time."

Daniels walked away from the window and tapped his foot. He checked his watch a second time. "Say, Jack, do you think I could get a drink of your panther piss?"

Tellum nodded. A bead of sweat ran down his bald head and settled on the bridge of his nose. He poured a glass of the ruddy brown liquor from his flask and handed it to Daniels. "This will put some hair on your liver."

Margaret began, "If you don't mind my asking—"

"Why would we mind you asking?" said Tellum with his obligatory menace.

"What is panther piss? It doesn't sound very refreshing."

Daniels said, "It's a bootleg whiskey, stronger than the real thing, right, Jack?"

"That's right."

Daniels drew a heavy breath. He raised the glass to Charles. "I suppose you could say I'm taking the piss, old boy."

The nephew only offered a curious befuddlement.

Daniels shouted as if Charles had not heard him. "I said, 'I'm going to take the piss.'"

Charles stuttered, "Cheers."

The lawyer closed his eyes and drank.

"Attaboy," said Tellum.

"Oooohh. No good. It's too sweet." Daniels went to the table and poured a glass of vodka from a decanter. He drank the entire glass in one gulp and then repeated the action twice more.

"Yeah, well, you need to relax. It's going to be a long weekend."

Daniels perched himself next to Charles and Margaret. "And here I thought I was Robert's best friend. You think you know everything about someone and then one day," he smiled at Tellum, "they have a few other chapters you've never read."

Margaret played with her necklace. "Mr. Tellum? You were joking, surely? You wouldn't have really killed that man?"

The toad regarded her without expression.

Daniels giggled. "Did you just clutch your pearls? We'll get Chuck a monocle to drop and you folks will be all set." He walked back to the window. "Jesus Christ, where is Rowan Manory?"

Margaret whispered in Charles's ear and they stood together. "If you gentlemen will excuse us, I think we'll go outside for a spot of fresh air."

"In this weather?" asked Daniels.

Charles laughed. "Oh, we're used to the rain. In England—"

"Yeah, well, don't go anywhere," said Tellum.

"We weren't planning on—"

"Just don't go anywhere."

"Of course not."

The couple held their smiles until they reached the hallway and then scurried to the left, out the front door, and onto the porch.

The rain showed no signs of stopping. It beat down heavily on the porch's metallic eave and created a rattling series of bangs.

Charles tugged his hair and stamped his feet. "Oh, God. Oh, Jesus. What have we done?"

Margaret stood perfectly still and spoke in a low, calm voice. "You're going to take it from a boil to a simmer, Charles. Don't ruin this for us."

He stumbled to the edge of the porch and stared past the ridge. The drowned remains of Vicksburg lay visible in the valley below. "I can't take it anymore. This was a terrible idea."

"It's a brilliant idea and we will go through with it. Listen to me." She turned him round, straightened his tie, and patted down the wrinkles on his collar with her long, smooth hands. "It's only a few more days. By

Tuesday, we'll be rid of Robert and we'll never see him or any of his friends again."

"We shouldn't have come. There's no way we'll get out alive."

"Look at me."

He lifted his eyes to meet hers. The light from the windows reflected faintly off her pupils.

"Have I ever led us astray?"

Charles took his wife's hand and kissed it. "Why can't we do it tonight? If I have to stay here three more days with these lunatics, I'll go crazy."

"Mad, Charles. You'll go mad."

"Did you hear the way he talked to me? If he catches on to us, it's all over. He has a gun."

"We can play it by ear. When the other guests arrive, we'll go to bed early and wait for an opportunity."

As the couple talked on the porch, their conversation could be faintly heard inside the billiard room.

Ruth Martice was in front of the window, listening as she calmly bit the skin around her fingernails. The secretary had been waiting for the Model T to arrive but now found herself intrigued by the drama playing out in front of her.

Tellum filled the billiard-room doorway. "You don't have to stand there looking out the window. Either he'll make it here or he won't."

She answered him without looking. "I just want everything to happen as planned. I don't want to disappoint Mr. Lasciva, that's all."

"Will Bernice be ready?"

She turned her head. "Aunt Bernice was quite tired when I left her, but I'm sure she'll be up for making an appearance tonight."

Tellum nodded and left.

Ruth put her left ring finger back in her mouth and ripped out the cuticle. She stared at the tiny wave of blood that swelled over her lunula.

Tellum's coughing reverberated through the hall. He pounded his chest and drew an arduous breath.

*Goddamn Paulie and his cigarettes.*

He waddled toward Lasciva's office at the back of the manor. After knocking on the door, he waited exactly ten seconds and then opened it.

Robert Lasciva drummed his misshapen fingers on the top of his desk and stared at Tellum. He turned his palms upward.

Tellum trapped a belch in his mouth and silently let it out. "Everything is ready. I don't know what else you expect from me."

"What are my nephew and his wife doing?"

"They went on the porch. Relax, they aren't going anywhere." A crackling noise came from the fireplace as sparks hit the wrought-iron screen. "Why do you have that thing going? It's so goddamned hot."

Lasciva pulled out a cigar cutter and put it next to a box of matches. "Where's Ruth?"

"She's in the billiard room staring out the window; hasn't moved for the last twenty minutes. Flighty dame."

"That's because she has a job to do and when she has a job to do, the job gets done."

"I'm doing my job, Bob. I can't make Manory drive any faster."

The cutter clicked on the end of a cigar. "Is Willie packed?"

"Are you going to ask me if I wiped my ass? What is this?"

"This weekend is very important to me." Lasciva struck a match and puffed the cigar until it was properly lit. He licked his teeth. "Is uhhh…is Bernice comfortable?"

"Yeah, well, you need to lighten up, boss. Paulie's in the library, Ruth's in the billiard room, the kids are on the porch, Bernice will be ready, and Willie can go screw. I still don't know why you need to have this dog and pony show. I could take care of this thing in five minutes." As Tellum turned to leave, the candlelight reflected off his sweat.

"Jack. You don't look so good. You aren't getting sick on me, are you?"

The bodyguard pulled out his flask. "This stuff will kill whatever bug I've got."

Tellum shut the door and had taken one step down the hall when it hit him. His sight blurred and he stumbled, reaching for the wall. He slumped to the floor and squeezed his hands. The pain started in his chest and crossed down to his stomach. He pictured it as a tidal wave and kept telling himself to ride it out. Finally, it abated. The sweat had formed a sheet over his skin.

"Are you okay, Mr. Tellum? Did you have too much to drink?" The voice came from the kitchen. It was Willie Aikes. The butler was leaning against the jamb; his head almost reached the top of the frame.

Tellum gasped and scrambled to his feet. He wiped his mouth with his sleeve and mangled his words a few times before saying intelligibly, "You packed, Aikes?"

"Yeah. I'm good to go, just waiting for this Chicago fella. He's sure taking his time getting here. You don't think something's happened to him?"

"After you show him to his room, I want you outta here. Understand?"

"Of course, Mr. Tellum."

He walked toward Willie and stopped a foot from him. "Don't you have anything better to do than stand there and gawk?"

"No, everything's done. I—"

"Then find something else to do. If I look at you too long, I'll have nightmares." Tellum smiled. "How's your brother doing?"

Willie's eyes darted toward the floor. "Jerry's fine."

"Yeah, well, tell him I said hello."

Willie backed into the dining room as Tellum coughed his way down the hall.

*I hope that turns out to be something serious, Mr. Tellum. I hope it turns out to be something you never recover from.*

Tellum composed himself before entering the library. "Are the limeys still outside?"

"You look like cold death," said Daniels.

"Yeah, well, I'm fine." He had another shot of panther piss. "He'll be here soon. Then we can get started and this nonsense will be over with."

The manor's appearance as Rowan and Walter came up the road had no resemblance to Walter Anderson's photographs in the Jackson museum. The fierce rain-soaked winds caused the spindly willow limbs to violently thrash, attempting to ward off any foolish visitors. In every window, the flicker of candle flames pulsated and created the illusion of movement.

*It is breathing.*

Walter shut off the engine a good twenty feet from the driveway. "How lovely. What do you think? Human experimentation? Satanic ritual?"

"Williams…"

"A wendigo?"

"Do you see? There are two people on the porch."

Backlit by the window of the billiard room, two silhouettes stood under the enormous eave. One of them gesticulated wildly and struck the other across the face. Both shadows then withdrew from the porch into the manor.

Walter said, "Trouble in paradise. What do you make of that?"

"Most interesting." Rowan looked among the ghostly trees and felt an undulating interior chill. "Eyes and ears open, Williams."

Walter started the car again and parked between a tan Studebaker and a red Fiat along the limestone drive. The detectives fetched the luggage from the trunk and ran through the hurling wind onto the porch.

The manor door creaked open.

Rows and rows of candles provided a warm glow to the hallway behind the five partygoers. Tellum, Daniels, Charles, and Margaret stood in a line.

Ruth Martice stood in front of them. "Is the weather this lovely back in Chicago?"

Rowan dropped his suitcase on the floor. "Not quite."

She extended her diminutive hand and he removed his sopping wet glove to grasp it. The prickly points of dead skin on her fingers raked against his flesh. "I'm glad you made it, Mr. Manory. We've been expecting you."

# CHAPTER 6

# FIRST IMPRESSIONS

*The easiest way to spot a fake smile is the absence of crow's feet. When one genuinely smiles, the orbicularis oculi muscle contracts and causes crow's feet to appear. The mouth speaks, but the eyes reveal so much more.*

It was Rowan's habit to size a person up as quickly as possible, providing both valuable insight and a testing ground for his powers of observation. In any event, it added a certain pleasure to the boring societal function of introducing oneself.

*Ruth Martice is the only one wearing a real smile. However, her dermatophagia would suggest she is perpetually nervous. From her unassuming black dress, I can infer that she cares not a whit about impressing anyone. Her limbs are tiny, but her frame is quite muscular and her eyes are much too large for her head. It is almost as if certain parts of her body ceased their growth while others continued unabated.*

*And what of the others? None of them are showing crow's feet. This is not a happy celebration. Are they upset that I am here or are they upset that they are here?*

*The nephew and his wife both have mid-Atlantic accents, but hers is far more pronounced than his. Charles seems to be literally dependent on her. Whenever she leaves him, his legs cross and he leans to one side. The word that comes to mind is 'feckless'.*

*When they are together, Margaret stands a bit in front of him. Even a moron like Tommy… Even a moron knows what that means. Did you slap Charles on the porch? I can believe he would not strike back. Look at those pearls. Good Lord.*

*At least they are trying to be friendly. Jack Tellum has refrained from offering even a fake smile. The man looks just like his mug shot from twenty-two years ago. His handshake hurts, and he is aware of this fact. He's probably even a bit proud of it. What is the gun in his holster?*

"Pardon me, Mr. Tellum. Which direction is the town of Jackson from here?"

Tellum pointed to the left without saying anything.

*That is a Colt Police Positive in his holster. He must have been given the gun by a department. I suppose he could have stolen it from an officer, but for some reason I think it was a gift.*

*Finally, there is the lawyer. Your face is flushed. Are you angry about something, Mr. Daniels? You sound like a swish, but I have heard that is not the case.*

"Did Ruth give you bad directions?" asked Daniels.

"What was that?"

"Is the house girl not doing her job? Is that why you and Mr.

Williams were late?"

"Not at all. The directions were from Robert."

"Of course. I forgot."

Tellum suppressed a cough. "Mr. Lasciva would like to have a word with you."

Ruth said, "Oh, Jack, there is plenty of time. These gentlemen have just had a very long and possibly dangerous drive."

"I'm just saying what was said to me."

Rowan eyed the drops of sweat on Tellum's forehead. "No need to worry. I look forward to speaking with him."

Walter took the opportunity to ask Margaret a question about England that he had long harbored. "What does your country do on the fourth of July?"

"Whatever do you mean? We do nothing."

"Is there a day of mourning? You see, we Americans have never really lost. We can't even imagine what it's like."

"What about the Alamo?"

"I'm afraid I don't remember the Alamo."

Margaret showed her crow's feet. Her laughter made its way down the hall of the manor.

And then…

Robert Lasciva opened his office door and strode down the long hallway with cocksure rhythm. The chitchat abated, leaving only the muffled sound of the rain and the creak of the wooden floor. All the guests faced him.

"It's been so long, Rowan," Lasciva said from the middle of the hallway. As he neared, his lime-green eyes looked down on the detective.

"Happy birthday, my friend. We forgot to bring you a present."

"Oh, I've gotten everything I wanted. My friends and family are here with me." He looked around. "Well, all except for Bernie."

"Who is Bernie?"

"My aunt Bernice. She's asleep upstairs. Don't worry, you'll get to meet her."

"Wonderful. In the meantime, Walter and I would love to change our clothes."

"I'll call the butler." He gave a lopsided grin. "I'm so glad you're here." Lasciva shouted down the hall. "Willie!"

Willie Aikes emerged from the dining room and lumbered down the hall. He took their bags and said, "This way, fellas."

As they passed the doorway to Lasciva's office, a cuckoo signaled nine o'clock. Willie led them up the detached spiral staircase to their room on the second floor.

Willie's protruding forehead caused permanent shadows over his sunken eyes. As the only Mississippian in the house, the butler's languorous drawl stood in sharp contrast to the clipped accents downstairs. "It's a comfortable room, sir. You'll be happy in here. You best keep the windows shut. I reckon the rain's not going to stop any time soon."

Rowan wound his pocket watch and sat on the edge of the bed. "Is this your room, William?"

"It's Willie, sir. Yes, it is."

"Where will you sleep tonight?"

"I'm staying with my brother. He lives down in Monroe."

"You are driving in this weather?" Just the thought of going on the road again caused Rowan's spine to spasm.

Walter frowned. "I could barely see five feet in front of the car."

"It's only about thirty miles, not a bad drive at all. Also, I've had about six months of driving in this rain. A fella gets used to things."

Rowan said, "Tell me, William—"

"Willie."

"Tell me, Willie, does Ruth Martice live here as well?"

"Oh yeah," Willie said. "Miss Martice has a room, Mr. Tellum too."

"Tellum is a full-time bodyguard?"

"Twenty-four hours a day. I can tell you right now, you don't want to cross him either. I seen some things that... Well, let's just say I seen some things. Mr. Tellum makes you feel like a long-tailed cat in a room full of rocking chairs."

Rowan rolled a cigarette and offered it to Willie. He graciously took it and the detective made a point to light it for him. "Does Paul Daniels live here too?"

"The lawyer fellow? No. He's got a house over in Clarksdale. That's the town where Miss Martice worked before she came here. That's how she got the job. Mr. Daniels used to spend quite a bit of time in the manor but not so much nowadays. This is the first time I've seen him here in quite a while."

Walter took note of Rowan's body language. With a country guy like Willie, Rowan took on a relaxed posture, nothing like the stuffed shirt that squeezed information from Delores Mcguinn, the debutante blackmailing her lover. It was also a far cry from the tiger that stood firm while Tommy Brent held a gun to his head.

"What can you tell me about the nephew and his wife?"

Willie's face scrunched up in confusion. "That's a funny thing. Mr. Lasciva never made mention of a nephew. I have worked here two years and three months and sure as Sunday he never brought it up. He told me we'd have two extra guests and said one of them was a nephew. That was the first I heard about it. In fact, it was the first time he said anything about any family. He never mentioned his Aunt Bernice, neither. Of course, I don't know nothing. I just work here is all."

Rowan cocked his head. "Oh yes, we did not get a chance to meet Madame Lasciva. Is she shy?"

"She's been in bed since noon, only comes down for lunch and sometimes an evening cocktail. Miss Martice says she's got some disease that makes her tired all the time." He opened his mouth to speak but reconsidered. "Nah. I shouldn't say it."

"William—"

"It's Willie."

"Willie, anything you tell me stays in this room. You have my word."

Willie smiled at the connection he felt. He rarely spoke this much to guests and Rowan's demeanor rang true. "I know I should be kind to a person that old but I can't help myself. She is the meanest snake in the grass I've ever met. And I've lived in Mississippi my whole life." Willie ducked his head into the upstairs hallway to make sure no one was listening. "She's German." He raised his eyebrows.

"Wait till she meets Manory. A more charming man will have never graced her presence," said Walter.

"No, Mr. Williams. I'm telling you she hates everyone and everything, especially Miss Martice. I can't figure it. Miss Martice is such a nice lady and that old woman calls her the filthiest names, stuff I wouldn't say to a longshoreman. Bernice was having lunch and Ruthie wasn't in the room. She asked Mr. Lasciva why he couldn't afford a prettier secretary. Miss Martice told me she says the same kind of things right to her face."

"A real charmer, huh?" said Walter.

"That's family for you," said Willie.

Rowan polished the scuffs on his shoes. "Just one last question. Has Mr. Lasciva ever mentioned Dorothy Roberts?"

Walter did a double take.

Willie shook his head. "No, I can't say he has. Of course I don't really know nothing."

"You just work here."

"That's right."

"You have been most helpful Will… Willie."

"If that's all, sir, I'd best be leaving. I'll be gone until Tuesday so we won't see each other again. But I want you to know, it's been a real pleasure." Willie paused for a moment and appeared deep in thought.

"What is it, Willie?"

"Oh, nothing, nothing. Just… Just watch yourselves while you're here. Keep an eye on each other?"

"Why would we have to do that?"

"Just remember what I said about Mr. Tellum."

Willie left and shut the door.

Walter squinted. "Why did you ask him that?"

"I asked him many things, Williams."

"About Dorothy, why did you ask him about Dorothy Roberts?"

Rowan ignored the question. "So, Lasciva and I will have a little chat. I'd like you to keep your eye on Charles and Margaret. Most likely it was the two of them that had the little scuffle on the porch. See if there is any tension lingering between them."

"No can do, boss. I talked to the nephew's wife while you were talking with Ruth. She and Charles are going to bed early."

"A pity."

"She did tell me something rather odd, though. She said to stay away from the panther piss. Said it was too sweet."

"What is panther piss?"

"I haven't the foggiest. I pretended to know so I wouldn't look stupid."

"Good work. You are a magnificent detective. Then play some billiards with Tellum and Daniels."

"Any theories on who wrote the note?"

"From handshakes and pleasantries? No."

"My money is on Tellum. Did you see his face? He's sweating like a whore in church."

"Where do you get these words from, Williams?"

"I heard the desk jockey say it when we picked up the car. When you travel to a new place, you have to use the lingo."

"The last Southerner has just left. You can drop the act."

# CHAPTER 7

# ROBERT LASCIVA

Robert Lasciva's smile was permanently crooked as the result of a fight during his teen years as a pickpocket; the bend in his bottom right gum forced one side of his mouth to rise while the other dropped perceptibly. This trademark was on full display as Rowan examined the office's centerpiece. The room had many conversation starters: the aforementioned cuckoo clock, a fifteenth-century Mandarin rug, and an original Thomas Hicks over the fireplace. Rowan, like the majority of Lasciva's guests, was immediately attracted to the most impressive item. Enclosed in a locked seven-foot-tall glass case was a suit of armor with a battle ax propped against the right leg.

Lasciva closed the office door. "It's centuries old. Paul tells me it's worth more than the whole house. I don't know about all that. I just like it when one of these pansy prohibition politicians comes to visit and I lock him in a room with a goddamn suit of armor. Then he knows I mean business."

Lasciva cachinnated until he wheezed. He was taller than Rowan by a foot and a half and his limbs made him look taller still. His stomach had ballooned a bit since his younger years, but it did not appear as fat. The detective had the impression that some as yet undetected cancer was brewing in there.

Rowan bent down and peered through the glass. "I would say 1400s, German." He frowned. "The weapon is wrong. This type of ax is for a mounted knight."

"So what?"

"The suit obviously belonged to a count. He would have had something stylish but ineffective."

"Maybe. Sure. When collecting antiques, one must sometimes mix and match."

"Also, the handle of the ax appears to be reconstructed. It looks like modern wood to my eyes."

Lasciva spread his arms wide. "I'm a bootlegger. I make my living passing things off as the original. Besides, I need a functioning ax." He wheezed another laugh.

"Of course." Rowan clasped his hands together. "Now, I did not come here to ogle your possessions, Mr. Lasciva. May I see the note you received?"

Robert's eyes lit up. "Yes, the reason you're here." He sat down at his desk and bade Rowan join him.

As Lasciva rifled through the top drawer, Rowan scanned the room. It seemed hermetically sealed. There were no windows to speak of and when the door was shut, all sounds of the storm ceased. The wood in the fireplace burned behind a crimson sofa. Rowan's gaze came to the flame's curlicue reflection on the oak floor. His eyes glazed over and the muscles of his face went slack.

*If the ghosts could only talk.*

A thwack of an envelope on his forearm broke the image's soothing hypnosis. He fumbled with the edges for a moment and then opened it. Inside was a half sheet of paper. He unfolded it and placed it on the desk. The detective read it once to himself and then aloud.

"Robert Lasciva. For debts owed and sins untold, you shall not live to be fifty-five years old. An old friend at the party shall end your life with a stroke so bold. Chip chop, chip chop." Rowan swallowed. "It is handwritten in cursive. Odd."

"Is there etiquette for these kinds of things?"

"Usually notes from criminals are typed or made with cut-up newspaper text so the handwriting cannot be recognized. Do you recognize the handwriting?"

"Nope."

"Has anyone else seen this?"

"Just Jack."

Rowan rolled a cigarette and reminded himself to keep a calm exterior. "Your nephew and his wife…"

"What about them?"

"Why are they British?"

"I thought you were a detective. They were born in England."

Rowan noted the lack of crow's feet when Lasciva offered his distorted smile. "You know what I mean."

Lasciva lit a cigar and puffed on it several times, creating a cloud of smoke that stuck to his head. "My sister, Ethel, went to England when she was a teenager. During her visit she got knocked up by a dashing young lad and decided to stay there. Charles was the kid. I got a letter from her every so often. She even sent me a picture of him." He flicked a photograph across the desk.

It was a young boy holding a cricket bat. Rowan flipped it over and read the writing on the back. *Charles nine*. Something pricked at his subconscious as if trying to iron out a wrinkle of relevant memory. It was his introduction to Charles earlier in the evening. Something that happened did not quite gel with this photo, but he could not say what it was and the feeling soon receded back under the rock from whence it came. "May I keep this?"

"It's yours, Manory." Lasciva leaned forward like a vulture without wings. "I wanted to tell you how sorry I was to hear about your mother. Damn shame. Damn shame about the Tommy Brent kerfuffle too. You win some and you lose some, right?"

Rowan did not look away.

Lasciva noticed. "I read about it in the paper. Immediately I asked myself where I heard the name 'Manory' before. Then it hit me. Your mother and I crossed paths briefly in Chicago, very briefly."

Rowan deemed it bait and decided not to bite. "When did you first meet Charles and his wife? In the flesh, I mean."

Lasciva leaned back and stuck the cigar in his mouth. "Wednesday."

"Wednesday?"

"Is there an echo? Wednesday. The kid wrote me in April. He told me Ethel died twelve years back. Now he was married and he was coming to America for a honeymoon with his wife. Charles wanted to meet his uncle."

Rowan's voice rose slightly. "Ruth Martice?"

"Paul recommended her. My old secretary quit in January. I do a lot of correspondence with business owners and certain high rollers. Somebody was needed for the job so…" From across the table he saw the detective's mouth was agape. "Did I fart?"

"I am sorry, Mr. Lasciva, but I am finding this more and more difficult to believe."

"What exactly are you having trouble with?"

"You receive a death threat. What do you do? You take in a long-lost relative and his wife, neither of whom you have ever met before. On top of that, you have a recently hired employee who has access to your home. She is your secretary?"

Lasciva shrugged his shoulders extravagantly. "Ruth is the last person I'm worried about. Look, Manory, I'm glad you're here. A man like me can never be too careful. However, the more I think about this situation, the more I'm inclined to believe it's all about money. I bet I get another note tomorrow demanding ten grand."

Rowan shook his head. "Where is your aunt right now?"

"I told you. Bernie's asleep."

"Did you only meet her recently?"

"I've known Bernie since I was wearing diapers. She's eighty and out of her mind for Christ's sake. There's no way she could do something like this. She doesn't even know what year it is. We have to keep reminding her. It's like a goddamn nursing home around here."

"Do you suspect your business associates?"

"I don't suspect. You suspect. That's how this works."

"Is there any other way to the manor besides the road? Could someone climb their way here?"

"I'd be impressed if someone tried to climb up this ridge just to kill me. I'd hire a guy like that."

"Are there any waterways?"

Lasciva took a pencil and paper from his desk and drew an outline of the ridge. "About sixty feet behind the garden, there's a clearing. An embankment runs parallel to the garden and then veers to the back. When it rains, the water collects on the mountain, and then runs through like a little creek. Of course it's a bit more than a creek now. No one could navigate it, though. No one would go up the mountain in this weather. There's too much danger of landslides."

Rowan looked at the note again. "Chip chop, chip chop. It is awfully familiar. I think it is from a nursery rhyme, no?"

Lasciva casually blew a ring of smoke. "I wouldn't know. I've never had a child."

Rowan bit. "Why did you leave Chicago?"

"I think you already know the answer to that question."

"I would like to hear it from you."

"I was accused of killing Dorothy Roberts. She was a girl I barely even knew. I met her at a club. She wanted to have a good time and I showed her one. She was," Lasciva twirled his finger next to his temple, "cuckoo. I've always been attracted to crackers. It's my great flaw. She jumped from a seven-story window. The police tried to pin it on me and it didn't work out so well for them. They got angry and then they got even."

"Why would she do such a thing to herself?"

"To see if she could fly? I don't know." Lasciva stood up. "I didn't hire you to solve a case from twenty years ago. What the hell does it have to do with this note?"

"Chip chop, chip chop! That is what Irene Roberts told the police after they found her raped and left for dead!"

Lasciva was speechless. There was no smile, fake or otherwise, on his face now. The skin hung completely loose as if detached from any muscle. Rowan was a bit shocked at seeing his reaction; it was human.

For a brief moment the two men stared at each other as if they had just met.

The cuckoo clock chimed a harsh combination of shrill metallic bangs and sharp bell chirps, breaking the silence in the office.

Lasciva licked his lips. "Well, that was exciting." He stubbed his cigar in the ashtray.

A knock came at the door. Lasciva mumbled to himself as he went to open it. It was Ruth Martice. At first, the secretary was beaming under her black Louise Brooks, but after a few words with Lasciva in the doorway, she took on his dour countenance.

Their brief exchange was too quiet for Rowan to hear, so he attempted to read Ruth's lips. Unfortunately, lip reading was a skill Rowan had been unable to master. He suspected this was due to his test subject. Walter mouthed words from across the office just fine, but the words themselves often turned out to be nonsensical gibberish that no one else could or would say in real life. Looking now, at Ruth's lips, Rowan made out only a single sentence. She definitely said the words, 'It was Jack.'

Lasciva turned back to the office. "We're being kicked out, Manory. Ruth has some work to do in the office and she can't have us running around like headless chickens."

Ruth sat in Lasciva's chair, her pale skin highlighting the freckles on her face. "I'm such a killjoy, I know. Please forgive me."

"Think nothing of it. I was hoping Robert would show me around the house anyway." When he reached the doorway, Rowan turned and nodded toward Ruth. She shoved three sticks of gum into her mouth and winked at him.

# CHAPTER 8

# MURDER

The hallway featured six oil paintings. Five were originals, but the one mounted next to the office door was a reproduction of *Judith Beheading Holofernes*. A Pavlovian shudder traveled through Rowan's body. He had first seen this painting in his parent's coffee table book. As a child, he had often dared himself to look at it.

*I would creep into the living room; it was important that no one saw me, for I could not explain this ritual. The Caravaggio was on page eighty-six. I opened to page eighty-five. My eyes closed and, in the comfort of the dark, I turned the page. I hovered above it for a while, trembling with anticipation. Finally, I would force myself to look. Judith's determined revulsion captivated me, but also made me fearful. This was my first glimpse into the savage capabilities of the human mind.*

"Coming, Manory?" Lasciva stood at the front end of the massive oblong hallway.

"Yes." Rowan shuffled his feet over the wooden floor, glancing at the other five paintings along the way. "You have exquisite taste in art."

"No, Paul has exquisite taste in art. Paul knows all. He tells me what's good, and I pay for it. It's like a marriage." Lasciva extended his right arm to the library. "Shall we?"

The ground floor consisted of six rooms. The billiard room, bathroom, and office were on the left side, while the library, kitchen, and dining room were on the right. Between the office and the dining room, the spiral staircase led to the upstairs bedrooms.

The burning lavender pastilles in the library replaced the stench of silt and wet earth that had settled in Rowan's nostrils. Shelves of books covered the entirety of the side wall. His eyes grew as wide as saucers.

"There must be a thousand." He reached forward without touching them. "Have you read them all?"

"Funny."

"It was not meant to be a joke. If I lived here, I would never accomplish anything. I would simply spend all my time immersed."

"It's just for show, Manory. I don't give a good goddamn about books." He caressed a section of red and yellow spines on the left-hand side. "I do like these, though. I always have time for a good murder mystery. You read them once and then they're no good anymore. I like that."

Rowan bent down to read the names. "Milne, Philpotts, Wallace, Van Dine, Leroux. They are not exactly giants of literature."

Lasciva appeared offended. "You're not a fan? This stuff should be right up your alley."

"That is why I am not a fan, Mr. Lasciva. None of these stories has a whiff of truth to them. The characters only act to present an impossible mystery for the reader. Real people kill for real reasons."

Lasciva wagged his finger at Rowan. "I think you just can't figure them out and that upsets you."

"I assure you, if any of these characters entered the real world they would behave much differently." Rowan stood up. "And I would catch them without much difficulty."

"Looks like I hired the right man. Come on, I'll show you the dining room."

Rowan took one last look before leaving.

*There are three front windows, but none on the side. Also, the dimensions seem smaller than they should be. Why is that?"*

Lasciva stuck his head back in the doorway. "Do you need help with anything?"

"No, I was just admiring your…" he looked to the corner of the room, "…phonograph. It is the old, hand-crank variety."

"It's junk, Manory. Let's go."

The dining room appeared cavernous compared to the library. A large, two-leaf table sat in the middle of the room and a towering cabinet loomed against the wall opposite the door.

*The cabinet's front shelves are only a third of its depth. Once again, the dimensions confuse me.*

He ran his palm along the thick side panel of the cabinet.

Lasciva said, "Ahh, you don't want to mess with that. It's an antique. You might break it. You'll have to pay me your salary and then some."

"And what if you are murdered? Who will pay my salary in that case?"

"I trust you won't let that happen."

"I solve murders, I do not prevent them."

"So I've heard." He pointed to two double doors on the side wall. "These lead to the kitchen. I didn't want an entrance from the hall, so this is the only way in."

Lasciva led him around the staircase, past the office doorway, and back toward the front of the manor, stopping only to show him the bathroom.

The last door was to the billiard room. Walter and Daniels were playing on the Medalist table. The room had six French windows, three facing the front of the house and three along the side wall. Rowan noted that the first front window had provided the light for the bickering silhouettes on the porch. Tellum sat next to the glass chess set, staring at the floor.

"Have you lost any money yet?" asked Rowan.

"Four," said Walter.

Daniels knocked in the nine-ball and straightened himself. "Five."

"I've only lost five dollars," said Walter. "I have him right where I want him."

Lasciva said, "Paul, be nice to the guests."

Daniels asked, "Have you shown Mr. Manory the paintings, yet?"

"No, I thought I'd leave that up to you. You're right, though. It's time."

Daniels put the cue on the table. "Shall we?"

Lasciva led Daniels and the detectives down the hallway to the Caravaggio next to Lasciva's office. "Rowan seemed enamored with our Jewish friend."

Daniels said, "Everyone loves Judith. She's—" His attention was drawn to the top of the stairs. "Bernice," he lisped.

The old woman slowly came down the steps. Her black arm-length gloves and matching evening gown made her head appear to float. It was a wrinkled head with a shock of white, frizzy hair. She looked at Robert through fat glasses. "We need to talk."

Rowan's heart skipped a beat.

*My God. It is a slightly younger Alice Schmidt. The accent, the hair, the glasses, an old German woman, the Caravaggio, chip chop, chip chop. It is all too much. What does it all mean?*

Lasciva hurried up the steps and tried to take her arm. "Easy does it, Bernie." As they descended, he motioned to the group. "These are my friends, Rowan and Walter. They just arrived this evening. You haven't met them yet."

"I don't like your friends, none of them."

"Of course you don't."

When they reached the bottom of the steps, Rowan and Walter bowed slightly. Bernice brushed them off with a wave of her small black hand and went straight into Robert's office. Lasciva followed her and the three men by the painting tried not to laugh.

"Like aunt, like nephew in this case," said Daniels.

"Maybe this will be the one for you, Williams. The woman you can finally settle down with," whispered Rowan.

"I do have a way with the crotchety and wrinkled," said Walter, waggling his brows.

The voices in the office became louder and the trio could not help but overhear.

"Madame Lasciva, I assure you there is no cause for concern," said Ruth.

"What do you know? You are not part of this family," said Bernice.

"You are right, but there isn't any danger of—"

"Ruth, don't worry. I can handle this," said Lasciva.

Bernice's shrill voice exploded. Every word snapped with indignation. "Handle what? Who is this woman?"

"Ruth is my secretary. I've already introduced you to her twice. You're pretending not to remember her just to give me trouble."

"Is she another one of your sluts?"

"Jesus," whispered Williams. "That's a bit harsh."

Paul Daniels tried to focus their attention on the painting. "It's a fascinating story. Judith was a widow who took it upon herself to seduce the general and kill him. She chose to behead him in order to impress her fellow Jews. Nothing quite succeeds like excess."

Rowan's eyes were on the painting, but he was not listening to Daniels. His ears were focused on the noises emanating from the office.

"Robert, if this house is searched, what will they find, I wonder?"

"Just watch it, Bernie. Don't forget, you're my guest."

"It's your home, Robert. You can bring in whatever trash you see fit."

Ruth's voice was now affected by tears. "Madame Lasciva, I hoped we could be friends."

"How dare you talk to me like this? You are nothing but a servant. Robert, I demand your help treat me with respect."

"Ruth, perhaps you'd better leave. You can finish the letters later. Go and clean the floors. They're wet from all the traffic," said Lasciva, a hint of desperation in his voice.

"Clean the floors?" asked Ruth.

"Yes. Be a good little girl and clean the floor. Versuchen sie nicht auf dem weg gefickt zu warden."

"That's not my job," said Ruth.

"Just go." said Robert.

There was a clanging sound in the room and then Ruth Martice came out with a bucket and sponge, her face fiery red. She stormed past the three men into the dining room.

Lasciva came out looking sheepish. "Christ this is embarrassing, huh? I mean damn. I'm sorry I—"

Rowan held up his hand. "No need to explain. We all understand the situation."

"When people get a certain age, they get cranky."

Daniels and Walter nodded in silent agreement. Ruth emerged from the dining room wearing a smock over her black dress and went straight into the library without looking Robert's way. Lasciva sighed and turned back toward his office. Before entering, he made eye contact with Rowan and gave him a grin. With the closing of the door, no sound could be heard from inside.

After this public display of drama, no one knew quite what to say.

Thunder grumbled from outside and Daniels audibly cleared his throat. "The rest of the paintings aren't as exciting as this one but I'd be happy to show them to you."

Rowan pointed to Walter. "Williams is the art connoisseur."

"I am?"

"Yes."

"Yes I am. I adore… art."

"If you will both excuse me, perhaps I can interest Mr. Tellum in a game of billiards."

Rowan left Daniels and Walter to the paintings in the hallway and made his way into the billiard room.

Jack Tellum was struggling to stand next to the table. His Kingsman suit was now drenched in sweat and the pink skin on his face had developed blotches of sickly white.

Rowan watched him for a few moments. Tellum did not seem to register the detective's presence. The toad grabbed a ball and banged it a few times on the table while staring at nothing. Rowan finally approached cautiously.

"Are you feeling quite all right, Jack?"

"Quite." The bodyguard pushed his tongue against the inside of his mouth and circled it. "Where's Bob?"

"Mr. Lasciva is in his office with his aunt."

"So, it's fine. It's started."

"What has started, Jack?"

Tellum urinated in his pants. "You'll see. I..."

The rain cascaded against the windows in waves as thunder boomed deep in the night sky.

Rowan continued on his path. "Jack, focus on my voice. If something is wrong, I want you to tell me before it is too late."

"I don't know what's happening to me, Manory."

Rowan gambled. "What happened to Irene?"

"Who?"

Rowan was inches from him. "Irene Roberts. The girl, Jack. Dorothy's daughter. Did you kill her?"

"Go screw."

"Listen to me, Jack. Whoever wrote the threat to Lasciva must know what you did. Chip chop, chip chop. Why else would that be in the threat?

"That's... That's impossible." What began as a laugh quickly sputtered into a hacking cough and then a full-fledged effort to breathe. His bulbous body collapsed to the floor and began a nauseating spasm.

"Williams!" Rowan tried to hold him still, but the sheer mass of Tellum stymied his efforts.

Walter and Daniels barreled across the hall. They stood stunned just inside the doorway.

Daniels said, "Good God, Jack!"

Walter ran to the table of liquor and poured a glass of vodka. Daniels intercepted his path to Tellum and smacked it from his hand.

"Don't give him alcohol. Go into the kitchen and get some water. The jugs are in the pantry."

Walter nodded. Fleeing into the hallway he saw Ruth in the library doorway and hurriedly said, "Something's wrong with Tellum."

Ruth ran into the billiard room and stood next to Daniels. "He's having a seizure. Put something in his mouth or he'll bite his tongue off," she said.

Tellum grabbed Rowan's lapels and glowered at him with bloodshot eyes as frothy spittle formed at the corners of his mouth. Ruth knelt beside them and tried to put the wet hem of her smock in his gritting teeth.

Walter came in with a glass of water, but tripped, shattering it on the floor.

"Christ, I'll get it myself," said Daniels.

"M-m-man-ory." Tellum tried to vocalize the words, but every syllable was followed by ungodly howls of agony.

"What, Jack?"

"This isn't right. It's a… it's a…"

"It's a what? Say it, Jack."

Tellum began to convulse. "Choke. Choke."

Ruth said, "Can't you see he's choking?" She forced the fabric into his mouth.

The toad's eyes widened as his muscles clenched. Then suddenly, Tellum ceased the struggle. The air hissed from his body and his grip on Rowan loosened. Blood oozed from his nose and drained off the sides of his cheeks as all his muscles slackened and the focus in his eyes deadened.

Charles and Margaret entered the room, still dressed in their evening clothes.

"Oh, God. What's wrong with him?" said Margaret.

"I believe he has been poisoned," said Rowan.

"It's the panther piss," said Margaret.

Rowan turned around in a fury. "What on God's green earth is panther piss?"

"It's the bootleg whiskey in his flask," said Charles.

"Did anyone else drink this piss?" asked Rowan.

"Yes!" said Charles. He pointed to the doorway where Daniels stood, holding a glass of water. "He took the piss!"

Ruth put her hand to Daniels's forehead. "Do you feel ill?"

He swallowed. "I'm perfectly fine."

Rowan searched Tellum's pockets. He pulled out a note. It was written in the same handwriting as the threat Lasciva had received. He read it aloud.

"Excellent work, detective. Two are now dead and without a single body as proof. Before the coming of the dawn, two more shall perish under this roof. Chip chop, chip chop." Rowan clenched the note. "Lasciva." He leapt off the ground and led the parade down the hall toward the office.

The knob failed to yield and he pounded on the door. "Lasciva, open the door! Bernice!"

Ruth said, "See if you can look through the keyhole."

Rowan knelt down. "I cannot. The key is in the lock."

Walter said, "Stand back." He stomped his foot near the lock. On the fourth kick, the door gave way just a little and on the fifth, it gave off a splintering sound. Finally, the door flung open and they poured into the room.

The suit of armor lay sprawled in the center of the office, bathed in a shallow but wide pool of blood. The top of the armor revealed the sinewy inside of a human neck. Three feet away, the helmet sat propped up with the ax by its side. Rowan crept toward it, the oak floor creaking under his feet mixing with the gasps of the witnesses behind him. He bent down and lifted the visor with his pinkie. Staring back at him, locked in an expression of utter astonishment, were the witless lime-green eyes of Robert Lasciva.

Ruth covered her open mouth and began crying. Charles held Margaret's head and averted his own gaze. Paul Daniels stood trembling near the desk.

Rowan pointed at Walter. "Williams, check the door."

Walter pulled it halfway closed and there, resting in the inside of the door, was the key. "It's here."

"His head is cut off," said Daniels.

"Where's Bernice?" said Ruth.

"His *head* is cut off," the lawyer repeated.

Charles fell to the floor, pulling Margaret with him. "I'm gonna be sick."

Rowan righted himself and began to roll a cigarette. "Everyone listen. You are all going to be calm, cool customers. I am a detective. Mr. Williams is my partner. We were hired by," he motioned to the decapitated corpse, "Mr Lasciva. We will get to the bottom of this and if you do as we say, no one else will get hurt."

The front door burst open and Willie Aikes's voice rang through the hall. "Mr. Lasciva."

Rowan motioned for them to leave the room. After everyone had filed into the back of the hall, he pocketed the key and swung the door closed.

Willie shouted as he stumbled toward them, his red raincoat

trickling water all along the floor. "The bridge is out. There's no way to get into town."

Rowan lifted his hand. "William—"

"He prefers Willie," said Walter.

"Willie, what do you mean?"

Aikes saw the shocked faces in front of him. "What's wrong? What happened?"

"You first, Willie. Go slowly and tell me everything."

He panted with his mouth open for a few moments and then began. "Mr. Williams was right. I couldn't see a damn thing out there. I'm always worried when I get to that little bridge after the loop, the Caddy's so heavy and all. She eased onto the first plank and then I knew I was in trouble 'cause there was no traction. I thought flooring it was the best idea. The whole thing gave way."

Charles backed against the wall. "It collapsed? There must be another way out."

"Quiet, Charles," said Rowan. "If the bridge collapsed, how did you survive?"

"I thought I was done for but I'll be goddamned if the car didn't fall perfectly. There are two rocky points in the crevice. The front end fell on one and the back on the other. I was just hanging there. I opened the door and climbed on the roof. Scariest thing I've ever done. I made it up the side of the ridge and when I looked down the Caddy slid off and disappeared. God musta been looking out for me."

Daniels pounded a cigarette on his case. "Musta been God. He's bent."

Aikes backed away. "I'm not... I'm... Why is everyone looking at me? Where's Mr. Lasciva?"

Rowan lit Daniels's cigarette. "How do we get out of here, Paul?"

Ruth answered. "We don't. That road is the only way out."

"Oh, God, we're stranded with a murderer," said Margaret.

"Who's a murderer?" asked Aikes.

Walter said, "What about visitors? If someone tries to come here they'll see the bridge is out and send help. Is anyone else coming? A mailman, a delivery boy, anybody?"

"There's a manager from the bank scheduled to come," said Ruth. "But—"

"But what?" asked Charles.

She flinched. "He's not coming until Tuesday."

Aikes screamed, "Someone tell me what's happening!"

Rowan placed the cigarette in the corner of his mouth. "Mr. Lasciva no longer requires your services. He has been murdered."

"Mr. Lasciva? Murdered? Are you sure?"

"Sure as Sunday, Willie."

# CHAPTER 9

# THE RIGHT QUESTIONS

Rowan stood next to the office wall and pressed his ear against it. He raised his left hand and gave two precise knocks on the wood. After waiting a few seconds, he shuffled two feet to the left and repeated the action.

In the fireplace, the embers glowed brilliantly through shadowed ash before receding. Red highlights bled along the logs' skeletal frames like lava oozing along the cracks in rock.

In the middle of the room, Lasciva's thirty-seven million cells continued to slowly break down.

Walter opened the door and set Tellum's flask on the desk along with a glass. "I parked them in the library. They're not thrilled with the arrangement."

"Neither am I. Did you find the gun?"

"What do you think?"

"I think you did not. If you had, you would have brought it with you."

"You've still got it, boss. Can't get anything past you."

"I suppose there's no sign of Bernice."

"Right again. I looked through all the upstairs rooms. Either she left the house or she's invisible." He pointed at the walls. "What are you doing?"

"Now and then, a mystery can be solved in seconds with very little work. I was hoping to find some walkway. I'm checking for a hollow sound."

"A secret passage?"

"Yes, a locked room without windows begs for another access point. Alas, there appears to be nothing."

"The situation is dire, isn't it?"

"Not at all. All mysteries are unraveled through concatenating. One action follows another and logically or illogically everything is linked."

Walter nodded his head a few times and then began shaking it. "The biggest mystery is why you keep me on as your assistant. I'm really no help to you. My head is swimming with questions right now."

"Applesauce, my friend. You are essential to my work. I have known it since our first collaboration and I am sure that this time will prove to be no different."

"You think I will solve this case?"

"No. I will solve this case. Your deduction skills are quite raw and you have a tendency to come up with pat conclusions, baffling motivations, and, quite frankly, backwards logic. But when I am struggling you always say something innocuous, a random thought that has nothing to do with the case. When you say this random thought, you light a flame inside of me. The flame burns and eventually it explodes into a brilliant realization. Every time this happens. It is uncanny."

"Have I lit your wick yet?"

"No, but you will. If you want to do something helpful in the meantime, you can look through Lasciva's desk." Rowan poked the ashes of the fireplace, searching for the remains of burned evidence.

While he flipped through the papers and other contents of the desk, Walter asked the questions he could no longer keep to himself. "If there is no secret passage and if there are no windows, how was the room locked from the inside? Where did the murderer go? Where is Bernice Lasciva and how did she leave this room? And why in God's name is he in a suit of armor?"

"Far too many questions to answer at once. Make it easy for me, my friend."

"Fine. Let's start with the locked door."

"The explanation of how the door was locked from the inside is not nearly as important as the fact that it *was* locked from the inside. Nevertheless, we shall amuse your curiosity. How do you think it could have been done?"

"Right." Walter cracked his knuckles. "Lasciva and Bernice go into this room and he locks the door."

"Did he lock the door?"

"I have to assume he locked it. It was locked when we tried to enter."

"Assume is a dirty word."

"What word should I use?"

"Asses assume. Detectives deduce."

"All right, I deduce he locked the door."

"It could have been locked by anyone at any time after he closed it."

"Fine, they enter and at some point the door is locked by someone. Bernice somehow vanishes and Robert Lasciva is beheaded in a suit of armor."

"Too many details. Simplify. There is a dead man in a locked room. What could be the explanation?"

"Suicide."

"Unlikely."

"Faked death."

"Highly unlikely."

"Monkeys."

"Monkeys?"

"Oh, yes. Monkeys can be trained to do anything. You've read Poe. You know, in Morocco, they train monkeys to—"

"I have been to Morocco. Monkeys did not chop off this man's head with an ax."

"The killer could still be in this room."

Rowan nodded. "This is a far more reasonable explanation. While you escorted our guests into the library, I performed a cursory search of the room. No one is under the desk or under the sofa or in the closet. There is no one here except our sundered host and us."

"He could have been killed after we entered the room."

Rowan wrinkled his nose. "Could he have?"

"Not in this case. I'm saying that in general it is a possibility. I read a story called *The Big Bow Mystery* where that happened. In the story, the detective breaks down the door and quietly slits the victim's throat."

"Williams."

"Did you do it, Manory?"

"This is one of those times I told you about."

"Sorry."

"Focus! What other solutions are possible?"

"I don't know. Ghosts?"

"A little bit of mystery and you head straight for the supernatural? Please, Williams, not on the first night."

"Do you know the answer?"

"I have better theories than yours."

Walter slapped a folder on the desk. "Do you care to share them with your partner?"

"I will wait until I have interviewed the guests. Then I can be sure."

"I see. Do you have a theory about where Bernice went?"

Rowan found nothing in the fireplace and sat opposite Walter at the desk. He opened the flask and poured two fingers' worth into the glass. "That is a much more troubling question. When Aikes told me that he had never heard mention of Bernice before, I was a bit suspicious of her. But everyone else seems to have met her. Lasciva himself said that he had known her since childhood. I do not believe people disappear, nor do I believe they walk through walls. I must deduce that Bernice is in this house, dead or alive. As for where she is or how she escaped this room, I am currently at a loss."

"She couldn't have lifted that ax."

Rowan wafted air from the top of the glass toward his nose. "I find Bernice to be a horrible distraction. A detective must battle distractions. The first questions we ask ourselves invariably end up being the wrong ones. A different view is often required. It would probably behoove us to concentrate on Lasciva. He had read about me in the newspaper. Obviously, it was the Brent case. So, think of it, Williams. You read about a detective causing the death of two innocent people and then you hire him when your life is on the line? No, no, no. The impression I got was that Robert Lasciva had no concerns for his own safety until…"

Walter waited a moment. "Until what?"

"Until I told him about Irene Roberts and the nursery rhyme. It unsettled him. Or at least it wiped the insufferable grin off his face."

"So did that." Walter gestured toward the disembodied head on the floor.

Rowan rose and shut the visor. He played with the corner of his cigarette paper as he paced.

Walter said, "How about the armor? Do you have any ideas?"

Rowan shook his head. "In the field of battle, one wears a suit of armor for protection. This is not a field of battle and obviously it failed to protect him."

"Perhaps the killer forced him into the armor. But why? It wouldn't serve any purpose."

"Putting on a suit of armor takes time even if one has practiced. He must have begun right after he closed the door. Whether Bernice forced him or he did it of his own volition, I do not know."

"Who else could have killed him? Ruth was in the library, Tellum was in the billiard room, and Daniels was with me in the hallway the entire time."

"Did Ruth ever leave the library?"

"No."

"Which painting were you looking at with Daniels?"

"The Forster. It's the one nearest the library door. She couldn't have slipped past me."

"She might have gone down the hallway after you and Daniels came into the billiard room."

"I doubt it. We were there less than a minute before I went back into the hallway to get the glass of water. I saw her in the library doorway. Her smock was still wet from washing the floor. So we must deduce that Lasciva was murdered when Daniels and I were looking at the painting and you were in the room with Tellum."

"He could have been killed just as Tellum was dying."

"So you think it was Bernice."

"Or the couple from upstairs."

"I guess Charles and Margaret had the opportunity, but I think I would have heard them coming down. Those stairs are terribly creaky. Anyway, none of this matters until we figure out how the door was locked from the inside. To lock a door from the inside, you must be inside. How do you leave a room and then put the key back in. It's impossible."

Rowan patted his shoulder. "Do not fret, Williams. It could be so much worse."

"Tell me one way this could be worse."

"There were two hundred and ninety-six murders in Chicago last year. Ten of them were decapitations."

"I find it troubling that you know this statistic by heart."

"Seven bodies were found and only three heads. None of the heads belonged to the bodies."

Walter smiled dumbly. "I understand all the words you just used. On their own they make perfect sense. It's just when you string them together like that…"

"The point is, heads are found without bodies and bodies are found without heads but we have got a body and a head and by the grace of God, they match."

"You're an awfully strange person, Manory."

Rowan pointed to the paperwork. "Anything interesting?"

A mountain of papers lay loose near Walter's arms, spreading in all directions. "Uhh…lots of manifests. The majority are shipments of coffin varnish. It's good to know bodies in Chicago are buried with style. You'd think the police would catch on." He stopped at a bound packet.

"Something pertinent?"

"It's Lasciva's will."

Rowan rushed to his side and pressed his fingers under the title of the first page. "Of course. Murdered bodies are often followed by the will." He skimmed through the document, looking for the good parts.

"Who gets what?"

"It is standard, very simple. The estate and all holdings are to be divided evenly between Paul Daniels, Jack Tellum, Charles Lasciva, and Bernice Lasciva. The witness is Ruth Martice. It is dated July fifteenth of this year." Rowan clucked his tongue.

"What's so interesting about that?"

"Don't you see? Robert put his nephew in his will before he had even met him. I would say this was not Robert Lasciva's style, but none of his actions seem to have followed any logical train of thought."

Walter's eyes bulged. "The note said two more would die. If Bernice is our man, Paul and Charles could be next. Let's not forget that there are two dead bodies."

"Trust me, I have not forgotten. Tellum died in my arms."

Walter pointed to the glass. "Is it spiked?"

"I could detect only the vaguest hint of alcohol. Otherwise there is no smell. With a name like 'panther piss', it should reek."

"Tellum was poisoned with something. Of that we can be sure."

Rowan shrugged. "Daniels drank from the same flask and he

shows no signs of sickness."

"Maybe he's just got to wait, the poor bastard." Walter imagined the terror of having poison inside him and just waiting for it to kick in. "Every small pain in his stomach must be horrifying."

Rowan finally lit the cigarette he'd been playing with. "How did the note get in Tellum's jacket?" He pulled out the two notes and laid them side by side on the desk. "It must have been planted earlier. It says that there will be no body as proof and yet, we have two bodies. Perhaps the killer planned to remove these bodies. Perhaps he still does."

"I have a good question." Walter paused. "I think."

"Please."

"Why is the second note addressed to you?"

"That is an excellent inquiry, my friend."

Walter smiled.

"My job here was meant to be a secret, but the killer knew. I think Jack Tellum knew as well. He was delirious when he died, but he was trying to tell me something. Ruth stuffed her dress in his mouth. Maybe she did not want him to speak."

"All he managed was the word 'choke.'"

"He was Lasciva's bodyguard. Why was he not constantly at his side?"

"I hope my last word is more meaningful than 'choke.'"

Rowan continued his pacing and rolled another cigarette while the previous one burned in the ashtray. "If Bernice had or has a motive of money then so do Daniels and Charles. Bernice also hinted that there was something in this house. Something that Robert would not want found."

"We haven't even mentioned Willie, he of the convenient bridge collapse. He could have been anywhere doing anything the whole time he was gone. Although I must say I have a good feeling about him. He seems trustworthy."

"No one is trustworthy," lectured Rowan. "Not now."

"Don't forget about Ruth. She was awfully angry when she left that office. I don't mean to cast aspersions, but when I saw her face, one word popped into my head."

"Murder?"

Walter tapped his nose. "That wouldn't look good in a court of law. Bernice also seemed to imply that Ruth and Lasciva were having an affair. She called her a slut and then said something in German."

"Do you speak German?"

"No."

"Good."

The cuckoo clock chimed, informing the men that it was eleven o'clock.

"Okay, Williams, I shall begin my interrogations. I imagine they will have to sleep soon, so I will be finished by midnight. While I am doing that, I want you to search the rooms more carefully."

"What is it I hope to find?"

"Something poisonous and a well-hidden Bernice would be very helpful. I—"

Walter screamed out a crazy garble of jitters. "Disgusting!"

"What?"

"Someone's left a huge wad of chewed gum under the table." He stretched it from his fingers and flicked it into the ashtray.

Rowan stubbed his old cigarette out and lit the new one. "I fear this will be a long night."

"Who do you want to see first?"

"Whom."

"Shouldn't you decide?"

"No, Williams. *Whom* do you want to see first?"

"Am I doing the interviews?" He grinned.

"Ruth. I want to see Ruth first."

"To which room should I send her?"

Rowan spread out his arms. "This one."

Walter stopped grinning. "You're going to interview them with a corpse on the floor?"

"Of course I am. What better way to get honest answers?"

"That's twisted. I like it." Walter poked his head out the door and looked both ways before leaving.

*How can he be so calm? His heart must be racing. His heart... I wonder if it will stand the pressure. You have to be an asset on this case, Walt. He needs your help. Remember, you're a professional.*

By the time Walter reached the library, he had steeled himself for confrontation. He raised his hand to knock on the library door and paused.

*That's not what someone in charge would do.*

He reached for the knob and pushed the door open.

All the guests were in the same place as when Walter had left them. Daniels stood smoking by the books as if he were allergic to sitting. Ruth sat next to Willie, holding a ripped piece of vodka-soaked smock against the scrape on his head. Charles and Margaret held their defensive position on the opposite sofa.

Walter began. "I'd like to express my gratitude for your cooperation. We've all been through a horrible experience but we're going to make it off this ridge if we stick together and remain civilized. Now, is anyone else feeling ill? Delirium, dizziness, anything like that?"

Willie scratched at the wound on his forehead. "Was he poisoned with the piss?"

"The answer is no," said Daniels.

"We are still determining the cause of death," said Walter.

"I knew Mr. Tellum sounded bad. He was hacking up a lung all the way down the hall. You all heard him. I'm not crazy."

Paul Daniels exhaled a large cloud of smoke and kicked the phonograph. "Since you're so clever, maybe you should go help Manory figure all this out. Hey, Williams, are you going to let all of this butler's brain power go to waste?"

Charles's hands trembled. "I don't think it's a good idea to keep us in the same room together. I mean, one of you is the killer. I'm not supposed to say it, I know, but it's true. Isn't it true?"

"Sure, Chuck," said Daniels.

"My name is Charles."

Ruth bit a small strip of skin from her ring finger. "What happened to Bernice?"

"That's the question, isn't it?" said Daniels.

"Aunt Bernice?" Charles forced a laugh. "You're right. She must have done it. An eighty-year-old woman did it. She cut off his head with an ax."

"I'm not saying Bernice did it," said Ruth. "I think it would be helpful to know what happened to her."

"Or her body," said Daniels.

Walter whistled until he had everyone's attention. "I have seen this so many times."

"You've seen what so many times?" asked Margaret.

"Panic. I'm not belittling any of you. It's human nature. Something happens that you cannot grasp and out of the cobwebs of the farthest corners of your imagination comes the fear of the unknown. The fear turns to panic and you turn on each other. But there's something you're all missing. Something I know that none of you could possibly be aware of."

"Oh, this should be good," said Daniels.

Walter pointed outside the door. "Down the hallway is the most brilliant deductive mind in the world. This is not hyperbole. There is no mystery Rowan Manory cannot solve. You are all very lucky that he is here. Right now everything seems lost and you feel helpless. By tomorrow morning, we will all know what happened."

The faces in the room did not seem especially comforted by Walter's words. He did his best impersonation of Rowan's walk and moved toward Ruth.

"Miss Martice, Mr. Manory would like the pleasure of your company."

Daniels leaned forward over the back of the sofa. "Why?"

Ruth stood. "It's all right, Paul. I'd be happy to provide any assistance." She took off her smock and walked out.

Walter followed her, but stopped and twirled round at the door. "Mr. Manory is now conducting his interviews. He'll be speaking to each of you in turn. In the meantime, I suggest you try to relax and keep your heads."

Daniels wore his sardonicism like  a second skin. "Smooth as silk, Williams."

# CHAPTER 10

# SUSPECTS

"Miss Martice, I understand this must be incredibly difficult for you."

Rowan had covered up Lasciva's body with a quilt from the closet and surrounded it with a few of Lasciva's dress shirts to soak up the gallon or so of blood that had spurted onto the oak floor. Ruth tried not to look but the seeping red patches were hypnotic. The fingers of her tiny, elfin hands were bitten to the raw, the undeveloped pink layer of flesh underneath contrasting painfully with her alabaster skin.

"I still can't believe it. How did this happen? Why?" She shook her head as the tears flowed freely, unencumbered by restraint. "It's revolting."

"It is unfortunate that the body cannot be removed, but my options are limited. I'm afraid it is now evidence."

"Yes, detective." Ruth struggled with a facial tissue, searching for a dry spot. After folding it three times, she gave up and placed it in the ashtray.

"In our present situation, it is vital that I ask some questions that may be of a personal nature. I hope you can understand."

"What would you like to know?"

Rowan momentarily fiddled with his cigarette and then lit it. "How did you come to be employed with Mr. Lasciva?"

"I came to Mississippi last October, but it wasn't for work."

"Where are you from?"

"Urbana."

"A fellow Illinoisan."

"Is that what we're called? I've never been called that." She removed her finger from her teeth and scrunched the hem of her dress. "The Red Cross set up a booth at the town fair. They showed pictures of what was happening here, and they told me about the levees breaking and all the homes being destroyed. It was heartbreaking. I volunteered."

"A very noble act."

"I had to do something. Also, I was still living with my parents. There's a point in everyone's life to forge out on their own. That was it for me."

"But eventually you—"

"Especially for the Negroes."

"The Negroes?"

"Why, yes. The government has come to the aid of white towns, but the Negroes have to fend for themselves. They have no assistance of any kind. It's shameful and it isn't right. I believe in justice, Mr. Manory. I've believed in it since I was a little girl."

"Yet you ended up here, above it all."

She hung her head. "I'm not as strong as I thought. I worked for a few months in the relief corps. Every week I would write home, saying I was fine. It wasn't the truth, though. Everything kept getting worse and worse. This flood is a losing battle. It just keeps raining."

The door opened and Walter stuck his head in. "Manory—"

"Not now, Williams."

"But—"

"Walter!"

Walter dropped his head and shut the door.

Rowan suppressed a frown. "I am so sorry. It keeps raining…"

"I gave my notice when I was stationed in Clarksdale. My plan was to go back home to be with my family. I felt like I'd given all I could. That's when I met Paul."

"Mr. Daniels?"

"Yes."

"Why was Paul Daniels in Clarksdale?"

"He lives there. We got to talking and he mentioned a friend who needed to hire a secretary. You must understand my situation. I was depressed and I had no money. I didn't want to go home a failure so I took the job."

"Ruth, I am not judging you. I cannot imagine what you have been through."

"That's good to know." She wiped her nose with the back of her hand.

Ruth's answers were satisfactory to Rowan but he cautioned himself not to be taken in by her apparent honesty. If a career in detective work had taught him anything it was this one simple fact: eventually, everyone lies.

"Were you and Mr. Lasciva having an affair?"

The question appeared to catch her off guard. She stammered a bit before answering. "How could you tell?"

*Forty-seven percent of employers have affairs with their secretaries, according to the Alfred-Dunning study of 1925.*

"Many things, Miss Martice. The way you stood close to him, your face, your body… your anger. Also, we heard the conversation between you and Lasciva's aunt."

"How embarrassing." She shifted in her seat.

"I told you there would be questions of a personal nature."

She rolled her eyes and then shut them. "I loved him and I think he loved me. One can never be sure though."

The thought of the diseased wretch touching her caused Rowan's mouth to go watery, like a prelude to vomit. He swallowed, kept up his smile, and nodded.

Ruth continued. "When I came here to work, it felt like home. Eventually, my role in the manor changed."

"How so?"

"Robert would have many parties here, almost every weekend. All kinds of people would come. Even with the flood, they would make the journey along the ridge. During Easter weekend, there was a rather large guest list and he was worried about handling such a large crowd. He asked me if I wouldn't mind greeting everyone and introducing people. I'm not the most sociable person, but I've done some work in the theatre. I know how to speak in front of a small crowd. The most difficult part was remembering everyone's name."

"You are quite talented at it. I can tell."

"It was the most fun I'd had in a long time. I met a lot of people, some real celebrities. Do you know the actress, Isa Bluette?"

He shook his head and laughed. "I am afraid I am permanently behind the times. Walter probably knows of her. He is much more culturally," Rowan searched for the word, "astute."

"She's a personal hero of mine and it was wonderful to get the chance to meet her. I also met David Devant."

"The magician?" Rowan perked up. "Yes, he is very good, a bit predictable but most entertaining."

"He pulled fifty eggs from an empty hat. I saw it with my own eyes."

Rowan finished her story. "Then he gave each egg to a volunteer who eventually could no longer hold them and they splattered on the floor."

"Exactly. You've seen him perform?"

"Indeed."

"The crowd was astounded. I think Robert was jealous of all the attention he got." She bit her bottom lip.

"I saw David Devant perform at the Balaban and Katz in Chicago. For the final act, he made an old woman disappear." The smile vanished from his face.

*Perhaps Mr. Devant could help us now.*

"After the party, Robert told me that he was impressed and he offered me a new job as permanent hostess. I still had to type letters and take dictation, but come the weekend, I was in charge." Her eyes sparkled through the gloss of tears. "It was like I was no longer an employee and then… We became involved. Do you need to know the details of how we became involved?"

"It is not necessary."

"As for my outburst this evening, you heard the reprehensible things Bernice said about me. When Robert refused to defend me, I felt betrayed. That's why I said what I said. There was no malice behind my words."

"Perfectly reasonable." He waited for her to speak again.

"We never discussed marriage. I'm sure he wouldn't rush into something like that because he isn't… He wasn't the impulsive type. He did say how nice it would be to finally settle down with someone." Ruth's pale pink lips trembled like those of a child and Rowan finally decided to hand her his handkerchief.

"Let us talk about Bernice Lasciva."

"Oh, let's not and simply say that we did." She managed to snort a laugh. "I don't know much about her."

"Did Robert ever mention her?"

"Only that she was his father's sister and she lived in Chicago. I was a little surprised when he invited her to come for his birthday, what with her never coming to visit before. Still, I was happy to meet some of his family. It seemed like a good opportunity to get closer to him. She took the train into Ashland on Tuesday, and Jack picked her up and brought her here. She had contempt for me from the moment we met."

"Why do you think she was especially venomous toward you?"

The tears seemed to disappear. "I think it's obvious. She viewed me as a threat."

"When the three of you were in the office, she seemed to imply there was something incriminating to be found in this house. Do you know to what she was referring?"

"I honestly don't, detective. She said lots of crazy things. You heard her. Have you any idea where she is now?"

Rowan sighed. "That is one of the many things I am trying to determine. I looked in the rooms down here and Walter is searching upstairs as we speak."

"I'm sorry for asking. I mean, they were together in this room and the door was locked but then she got out somehow but the key was still inside. I'm just so bewildered."

"As are we all, Miss Martice." Rowan rose from the desk and began his customary pacing back and forth. "Did Lasciva talk much about Charles?"

"No, not until the letter came. He didn't know what had become of his sister or her son."

"What was his reaction when he received the letter?"

"He was delighted. He had assumed Ethel was deceased because she stopped writing him but now was happy to get the chance to start a relationship with his nephew. I think Robert liked the fact that some part of his sister was still alive."

"I find it very hard to imagine Robert Lasciva as a caring man."

"Obviously you didn't know him very well. He loved Ethel and he wanted to have a relationship with Charles."

Rowan cast a doubtful glance at her. "We found Robert's will. He included Charles as a beneficiary."

"That should tell you how he felt."

"However, you are not a beneficiary."

"I'm not here for money, Mr. Manory."

Rowan combed his hair with his fingers. "Did you get along with Jack Tellum?"

Ruth laughed again but derisively this time. "Oh, no. No one got along with Jack Tellum. He was always here, but I tried to avoid him whenever possible. I know that Jack and Paul were old friends of Robert's, but I never really dealt with them."

"But you said before that you knew Paul. You met him in Clarksdale."

"Yes, but our interaction was brief. I think he was sweet on me. He's a nice enough fellow but... you know."

"Do you think he was angry that you ended up with Robert?"

"Not angry enough to do this."

"Could Willie have done this?"

"Everyone gets along with Willie. He wouldn't hurt a fly."

"Ruth, did anything strange happen this evening?"

She stared at him blankly.

"I mean before this." He motioned to the bloody quilt. "Before I arrived, was there anything out of the ordinary?"

"Yes. Charles and Margaret had a row on the front porch. I was in the billiard room waiting for your arrival and I saw them."

Rowan perked up again. "You saw them through the window?"

"Yes, I was standing right in front of it."

"Why were they fighting?"

"I didn't hear everything clearly but I caught the gist of it. Charles was unhinged, stomping around the porch like a madman. Margaret told him not to be a wet blanket. She felt like he was being rude. He was complaining that everyone in the manor was strange and that coming here was a mistake. But then," Ruth's eyes became impossibly big, "she said that they would be rid of Robert by Tuesday and would never see him again. I had the impression she meant they would leave and never come back, not that he would be dead. I want to make that clear."

"Did you watch them come back in the house?"

"Yes."

"From the window?"

"Yes."

"Nothing else happened?"

"No." She looked confused.

Rowan ground his teeth. "Just one more question. What did you do with Tellum's gun?"

Her head turned to the left. Though they were in the office, she seemed to be imagining the billiard room in front of her. "I took it from his pocket and then I put it on the ground near the window. I didn't even think about it. It could have gone off while he was shaking like that. Can't you find it?"

"No. Williams checked the billiard room and it is nowhere to be found."

"That's not good, is it, detective?"

"It is nothing to worry about. I am certain it will turn up somewhere. Thank you, Miss Martice. Kindly return to the library." Rowan waited for her to reach the door. "Oh, I forgot. I did not want to embarrass you, but we found your gum."

Her ghostly face whipped around. "My gum?"

"Yes. It was under the desk."

"I suppose it's very unladylike. We all have bad habits."

She left the room and Rowan eased into the chair.

*Some of us are worse than others.*

Walter cracked open the door. "Am I allowed to enter?"

"That depends. Have you found anything?"

"No Bernice and no poison but you won't believe what I did find."

Rowan waited for him to speak but Walter remained silent. "For God's sake, Williams."

Walter grinned like a schoolboy. "I was searching Tellum's room. It smells like lavender if you can believe it."

The detective held his head in his hands.

"Right, right. I opened the first door of his desk and found this." He held up a wallet and placed it in front of Rowan. "Have a look inside."

Rowan opened the wallet and searched through its contents. He stopped at a written list of businesses with various account information including outstanding debts. "What is the importance of this, Williams?"

"Look at the way the t's are crossed."

Rowan's eyes followed the peculiar upward slant on the letter. Recognition dawned on his face. He put the list next to the two notes. "The handwriting is exactly the same."

The grin remained plastered on Walter's face. "Do you realize what this means?"

"Yes. It means that Jack Tellum was the author of the threat sent to Lasciva and of the taunting note addressed to me."

"It means I was right, old man. I told you that Tellum had written the threat."

"Surely you can recognize a lucky guess when you see it."

"But what does it mean? Where does it leave us?"

"I do not know, Williams. It is certainly not what I had expected. Go and fetch Charles."

As Rowan eased back in the chair behind the desk, he felt the cool calm of certainty. This particular imbroglio was a fine challenge for his wits but was by no means an albatross. Even a million-piece puzzle could be solved if he managed to collect all its pieces and decide on their place. Rowan lit a cigarette.

*Tellum wrote the threat.*

Charles entered and sat down. Rowan watched as he ran his fingers through his wavy hair and pulled on the sleeves of his houndstooth suit. Rowan estimated it was too small by at least three sizes. The younger Lasciva was boyishly built. A middling-sized man, he resembled Daniels sans the thinning hair, wit, and lisp.

Charles shifted his gaze from Rowan to Walter to the corpse and then back again. Without any prompting, the nephew began to recount the events of the evening. "I was asleep in my room... with my wife, naturally. We heard shouting and we came down the stairs. It was impossible to tell what was going on, so we were extremely cautious. I saw Paul Daniels go into the kitchen and we went straight to the billiard room—"

Rowan cut him off. "Mr. Lasciva, there is no need for this."

Charles seemed flustered. "Don't you want to know what I saw?"

"Not particularly."

In the silence after Rowan spoke, the younger Lasciva fidgeted. "Then why did Mr. Williams ask me in?"

"I need to find out who wrote the note in Jack Tellum's pocket. What I need from you is a sample of your handwriting to see if it matches."

Charles cocked his head and blinked. "Yes, of course. Not a problem." His demeanor transformed. "I'm positive I didn't write any note."

"Excellent." Rowan put paper and pen in front of him.

"What would you like me to write?" asked Charles.

"Your signature will be sufficient."

He quickly signed. "Anything else?"

"This panther piss you saw Daniels drink - was there anything odd about his behavior when he drank it? Did he seem unduly nervous?"

Charles nodded confidently. "Before he drank it he said he was going to take the piss. He said it twice. Then, after he drank it, he consumed two... no, three full glasses of vodka. Quite strange, don't you think?"

"Oh, yes, Mr. Lasciva. It is very strange. Where in England are you from?"

"I grew up in London, but we moved to Chichester when I was six. It's in the—"

"I know exactly where it is. Your mother, Anne, when did she pass away?"

Charles pulled at his sleeve. "Her name was Ethel."

"Oh, yes. I'm terribly sorry. When did Ethel pass away?"

"She died in 1915."

Rowan nodded. "Right, right. What did you do with yourself after your mother passed?"

"You know, a bit of this and a bit of that. My father took care of me."

"What happened to him?"

"He died of Legionnaires' disease. It must have been seven years back. I didn't have much money so I worked on a fishing boat. That's when I met Margaret. Her family is quite wealthy. They own a lot of the fishing boats in Chichester."

"I see. Why did you wait such a long time before contacting your uncle? Would it not have made more sense to contact him directly after your mother had passed?"

"I didn't know him. I'd never met the man. When I told Margaret about my family history, she convinced me to make some phone calls and eventually we discovered where Robert lived. We had always planned a honeymoon in America, so it seemed natural to come and meet him, and he was rather receptive to the idea."

"He was not what you had expected, was he?"

His face went blank. "No. Nothing about this trip has been what I expected."

"When did you and your wife arrive in Mississippi?"

Charles's eyes rolled up as he tried to picture the days on a calendar. "Let's see, we came here on Wednesday."

"So your grandaunt had already arrived?"

"Bernice? Yes, she was here."

"Did you speak with her?"

"A little. We had lunch on Thursday and earlier today. She's not a very pleasant woman." Charles looked at the outline of his uncle's body. "Do you know what happened to her?"

Rowan narrowed his eyes at the nephew and slowly pronounced his words. "I will know in due time. Thank you, Charles. Please go back to the library and ask your wife to join us."

Charles stood with evident relief and shook both Rowan and Walter's hands. "If you need anything else, don't hesitate to ask."

He left the room and Rowan crumpled the signed paper and threw it in the trash without looking at it.

Walter threw his arms into the air. "I'm just going to stop asking you questions."

Rowan lifted the tissue from the ashtray and focused on the gum.

"I want you to grab one of the raincoats from the rack in the hallway and go out to the cars. Daniels has a Studebaker and Charles, the Fiat. See if there is anything in the back seats."

"Am I still looking for Bernice or something poisonous?"

"Anything."

Rowan laid the will on the table and stared at it.

*What if the puzzle pieces are blurry? No worries, old man. Everything happens for a reason. Once you know the why, the how is easy.*

His heartbeat echoed for a second and he waited for it to realign.

Margaret Lasciva pleated her skirt as she entered the room. She showed none of the tears that Ruth had displayed or the nervousness of her husband. Instead, her face was a round chilled image of composure, save for the mascara smudges under her eyes from excessive rubbing. Her blonde hair was coiled in a simple bun around the back of her head. Rowan waited for her to sit and then immediately pointed at her necklace.

"Do you sleep in your necklace?"

"It's a habit. I reach for it the moment my feet hit the floor."

"Those are lovely pearls." He moved in for a closer look. "They are flawless. Extraordinary."

"A gift from my mother." She moved two of the pearls back and forth with her fingers while she spoke.

"Do you also sleep in your dress?"

"I threw it on quickly. I can't imagine being seen in my pajamas by people I barely know."

"Your husband even took the time to throw on his tie."

"Mr. Manory, is there a murderer in the library right now?"

"I hope not, Mrs. Lasciva, but there very well might be."

"I suppose you deal with murderers all the time in your line of work."

"Not as often as you suppose."

"Well, I have never been in a situation like this. Charles and I only wanted to spend some time with his family. This was supposed to be our honeymoon." Her eyes drifted to the floor. "What is it you would like to know from me?"

Rowan asked her the same questions he had asked Charles and she gave the same answers. She went on a bit about her family and Rowan allowed her to continue before getting to his real questions.

"Are you angry with your husband?"

"With Charles? Not at all."

"Do you quarrel regularly?"

"Yes, about his bloody addiction to boiled sweets. Mr. Manory, we are the same as any other couple. Occasionally we have an argument."

"You had an argument earlier this evening on the porch, did you not?"

Her jaw dropped. "I wouldn't have called it an argument. It was a discussion. Who told you this? Was it Ruth?"

"Did you strike your husband when you were on the porch?"

"I have never hit Charles, not once. And he has never hit me. Did she tell you otherwise?"

"No, Mrs. Lasciva, she did not. What was it you were discussing?"

Slight panic showed in the quivering corners of her mouth. "We didn't feel quite comfortable here."

"Why not?"

"Where to begin?" Her tone changed from defensive to assured with startling speed. "I could start with Paul Daniels. The more polite you are to the man, the snider and more condescending he becomes. And Bernice..." Her face turned smug. "Did you have the pleasure of meeting her before she vanished?"

"Very briefly."

"Then I don't have to say another word, do I?" Her voice rattled with barely concealed mania. "Robert invited us here and yet he was cold and distant. Ruth makes herself out to be agreeable and diplomatic, but I know her type, Mr. Manory. Behind her façade she plays people against each other for her own amusement."

"How do you know that?"

"And then there is Mr. Tellum. Before Charles and I went out to the porch, he had been regaling us with an oh-so-charming story about threatening a man with a crowbar."

"Whom?"

"The butler's brother."

"Tellum threatened Willie's brother? Why would he do a thing like that?" Rowan leaned forward.

"Apparently Willie's brother purchases alcohol from Robert and then sells it. How do you call it? A distributor." She glanced at the bloody quilt. "I suppose he *used* to purchase it from Robert. There was some dispute about the price and Jack was going to kill him when he complained. He was going to do it with a crowbar, no less. It's frightening to meet a real person who does those kinds of things. Charles was shaken up and I had to calm him down. He's a gentle man who doesn't react very well to violence. That's all. It was not a fight."

"I see." Rowan paused for a long time as Margaret caught her breath. "One last question. Have you ever been in the theatre?"

"When I was younger. What has that to do with our present situation?"

"Just wondering. Thank you for your assistance. If you would be so kind, please tell Mr. Aikes that I would like to see him."

"Mr. Manory?"

"Yes, Margaret?"

"I'm far less worried about you suspecting Charles and myself of this crime than I am about us being murdered tonight." She tightened her jaw, attempting to keep the tears welled in her eyes. One escaped down her cheek.

"I know. Nothing will happen to you. I promise."

"Did you make the same promise to Robert?"

"No, I did not."

She quickly composed herself and left the room.

Rowan drummed his fingers on the desk.

*Why do we start with the pinky when we drum our fingers?*

He awkwardly began with his index finger.

*It rings false. You can tell when things ring false. All that is needed is a pair of ears and half a brain. Three suspects and three liars.*

Rowan once again became aware of his heart. It had not bothered him since the car ride, but he knew it to be a ticking time bomb that could go off at the most inopportune moment.

Willie held a towel to his head as he tottered across the office. "Christ, will you look at that." He motioned toward the bloody quilt.

"I have been looking at it. Are you feeling better, Mr. Aikes?"

Willie did not answer straight away. The man sitting in Robert Lasciva's chair was not the same person who had been so friendly earlier in the evening. The only person who called him Mr. Aikes was the eighteen-year-old who delivered the jerky once a month. "Uh huh. I'm tired but I'll survive."

"I am going to ask you some questions. Hopefully, you are going to tell me the truth. What was your brother's relationship with Robert Lasciva?"

"My brother didn't exactly have a relationship with Mr. Lasciva. He did some business with him."

"Why did Jack Tellum threaten your brother with a crowbar?"

"Oh no, you're barking up the wrong tree, Mr. Manory. My brother bought alcohol from time to time, same as a hundred other folks in a hundred other towns around here. Now, I told you about Jack Tellum. I spoke the truth when I did. He was a nasty fella."

"I agree. However, I am inclined to believe that your brother was threatened for a reason."

"Probably, but I don't know nothing about it. I just—"

"Work here. You just work here." The detective surprised himself with his sarcastic tone. His heart beat against his breastbone and he chewed on the inside of his cheek. "We will try an easy question. How long were Ruth and Robert involved?"

"Ruthie and him didn't go together."

"They were lovers, Mr. Aikes."

"I hate to sound like a broken cylinder but I don't know nothing

160

about that."

"Do not treat me like some Catholic bog hopper. I know they were having an affair."

"And I'm telling you they weren't. She had some fella where she came from."

"William—"

"It's Willie."

Rowan erupted from his seat and scowled as he paced like a caged lion.

"What's wrong with you, Mr. Manory? I'm being as straight with you as I can."

Rowan nodded. "I am sorry, Willie. This is turning into a frustrating evening."

Willie spoke with a conciliatory tone. "Maybe they were together, Mr. Manory. If they were, they sure kept it a secret. Ruth doesn't talk much about herself, but she did say she had a fella that she was sweet on in Clarksdale."

"And your brother?"

"Jerry's got a smart mouth and it gets him into a lot of trouble sometimes. He and Mr. Tellum didn't get along very well, but nothing so bad I would have to kill Mr. Lasciva because of it."

"I have not accused you of killing Mr. Lasciva."

"Their business never concerned me. I stayed out of it."

"Criminal activity tends to bring out the worst in people."

Willie sighed. "You have to understand. Things here aren't like in Chicago. Selling liquor here isn't such a big deal. We don't kill each other over it. We just drink it and enjoy ourselves."

"Thank you. You can go."

"Should I send in Mr. Daniels?"

"No."

Willie left the room, keeping the door open. The thunder from outside filtered through the hall. Rowan looked down at the quilt and addressed the corpse directly. "What the hell were you up to? It would all make sense if not for you. You do not make sense, Mr. Lasciva. If you do not say the things you said everything is solved."

*Stop talking to a dead man.*

Walter entered, wet and shaking his head. "No Bernice. Charles has some tools in the back seat." He shut the door and stood next to Manory. "Do you know what the kids call the back seat these days?"

"Williams—"

"A struggle buggy. Can you guess why?"

"Which tools, Williams?" Rowan was serious.

"Hammer, saw, chisel, gimlet, nothing out of the ordinary."

"Subtle. What about Daniels's Studebaker?"

"Things you would expect to find in a car. He has a map. I couldn't see very well, but I think it's of Mississippi. He has antifreeze, Eveready Prestone, the same kind we buy. There's a suitcase, a tire iron, and a jack."

"Good work. Let us go to the library, my friend."

Rowan considered his next move carefully as he passed the paintings. His instincts were rarely misleading, but the Tommy Brent case gnawed at him and shaded all his thoughts with doubt.

*Chip chop, chip chop.*

Rowan looked over the suspects. "Ladies and gentlemen, I know everyone is frightened. Trust me when I say that Walter and I are as well. It is getting late and I think it best if everyone got some sleep."

"This is the brilliant mind we've heard so much about?" said Daniels.

Charles gritted his teeth. "How am I supposed to sleep? Who do you think the killer is?"

"Whom," said Walter.

Rowan said, "Come now. In the morning, we will all have clearer heads and we can decide on a suitable course of action. Mr. Aikes, as I understand it, each bedroom has its own key?"

Willie nodded. "That's right, sir. Everyone here knows the keys are hung on a latch inside the room."

"Splendid. I want everyone to lock the doors to their bedrooms and not to open them for anyone, including Williams and me. Mr. Daniels," he put his hand on Daniels's shoulder, causing him to twitch, "I would like a quick word with you alone."

Ruth stood up. "I'll have to put out the candles. If the storm breaks one of the windows, it could knock them over and start a fire."

Walter asked, "Are there any flashlights in the house?"

"No, we operate by candlelight," said Willie.

Rowan chuckled. "All right. Charles, Margaret, and Willie, please accompany Ruth so she is not left alone. We will see to the candles in this room. After you are finished, I want everyone to go straight to their bedrooms."

They exited the library and Rowan lit the cigarette that he had carried down the hallway.

Daniels poured himself a vodka. He circled the rim of the glass with his middle finger.

Rowan asked, "Why did Lasciva keep the threat a secret from you?"

"You would have to bring him back to life and ask him. Do you have any notion of who was behind it?"

Rowan shook his head. "It could have been anyone who had grievance with him."

"I'm afraid you will have an extensive list of suspects."

"I can imagine. Mr. Daniels, before this week, had you any previous knowledge of Bernice Lasciva?"

The lawyer jutted his lower lip and nodded his head. "Robert talked about her a lot. He had a soft spot for his aunt. She was an immigrant who came here with nothing, you know, the all-American story. I first met her years ago in Chicago."

"What about Charles and Margaret?"

"Not really. I knew Robert had a nephew, but that was all. I had no idea the boy was married." Daniels paced through the room and spun the mandrel of the phonograph. "How did Bernice do it?"

"How did she do what?"

"Don't be coy. How did she kill my best friends and then vanish from a locked room?"

"I do not think she did."

"I suppose you think I did it? That's why you wanted to talk to me alone? Maybe you can explain how I managed to kill Robert in the office while I was talking to Walter in the hallway. That's a hell of a trick."

*You are sweating like a whore in church.*

"Mr. Daniels, when we broke into the office and saw Robert's condition, you said his head had been cut off. In fact, you said it twice. Why?"

"I think it was a fairly apt description."

"Yes, but you did not say, 'My friend is dead,' you specifically said his head had been cut off."

"Is there etiquette for these kinds of things?"

"That is the second time I have been asked that question tonight." Rowan smiled at Walter.

"So what if I said it. I didn't think about what to say. I was genuinely taken aback."

"Oh, I believe you."

"What does it prove?"

"Nothing at all, Paul. I was simply curious. I wanted to talk with you alone because I did not want Willie in the room."

"Willie?"

Rowan nodded. "That is right. It would make sense. Think about it. He was gone when Lasciva was murdered and could have hidden somewhere in the house. You were in the hallway, Margaret and Charles in the bedroom, Ruth in the library, and I was with Tellum. As the butler, Willie would have access to the liquor in the house."

"What about Bernice?" Daniels drank the vodka in his glass in a single gulp.

"Until I figure out what happened to her, I must work with the people who are here."

"What are you going to do next?"

"Williams and I are going to drive to the bridge and see if it has, in fact, collapsed. If it has not, then Willie will have to answer for quite a bit. I need you to be watchful, Paul. Stay awake while we are gone and tell me if Willie leaves his room." He inhaled deeply on his cigarette. "The helmet Robert was wearing has a back plate that covers the neck."

"This is significant somehow?"

"It means the killer cut off his head and then put it inside the helmet afterward. Think about the effort for such a useless effect. We are dealing with a psychopath, someone who is operating on pure malice. There is no rationality to be found within this murderer. As you said, Robert's *head* was cut off."

Daniels lost a shade of his color as his mouth went dry and he said rather quickly, "Good night."

"Good night, Mr. Daniels."

Daniels left the room and caught up with the others as they blew out the candles and the manor grew darker and darker.

Walter said, "Manory, are we really driving to the bridge?"

"No, Williams. We are driving just out of sight, about fifty feet past the start of the forest. Then we will walk around the trees, and go to the river and wait."

"Wait for what?"

"With no way off this ridge, I suspect our murderer is beginning to panic just about now. Whatever plan was in place must be altered. Bernice Lasciva was meant to provide a distraction. Her disappearance would naturally make her a suspect. In order to keep this possibility alive, her body would have to be removed from the manor. The river would be the most logical place. Normally, it is just a tiny creek. With the current rainfall, it is over six feet deep and rapidly flowing. The corpse will be taken quickly by the current and dumped into the ocean of water covering Vicksburg."

"Why did you tell Daniels we were going to the bridge?"

"Do you know the average temperature in Mississippi?"

"Not offhand."

"Hot."

# CHAPTER 11

# THE RIVER

The moonlight pierced through the uninviting, pitch-black curtain draped over the sky, and a fine constant mist replaced the heavy rain. Walter walked down from the porch and turned his face upward. His shoulders dropped and a goosebumped calm took over his body. The whistles of the wind, waffling between gust and breeze, gossiped with the rustling willow branches.

He called back to the opened manor door. "Manory, I think it's stopping. The rain is—"

Without warning, the weather summoned all of its strength for a monumental display of authority. Walter's raincoat hood blew back and torrents of rain lashed at his exposed face. He wiped the sting from his eyes and a crack of thunder pierced his eardrums. Panicked, he fought his way toward a hazy pixilated image of the Model T. With a slam of the door, nature's fury was muted. Only the rattle on the car's surface accompanied the sound of his labored breathing.

In the isolation of the car and with a rush of adrenalin, Walter contemplated his situation.

*I'm alone, trapped on this ridge. There is an unknown killer creeping round somewhere.*

He thought he saw something in the side mirror and twisted his body to get a better look.

*The butcher could be anywhere. Of course, if he is crawling on his belly beside the car about to jump up and slit my throat, he must be awfully uncomfortable.*

Walter laughed for a moment at the thought of a killer experiencing discomfort like a normal person. This led to thoughts of a murderer struggling with a jar of olives or experiencing a flat tire.

*Why wouldn't a murderer experience a flat tire? That's just silliness. The fact that he killed someone would have no bearing on basic tire maintenance. Why, this man must go through everything life has to offer. He has to wait in line at the post office and send Christmas cards to his relatives. I wonder if they suspect anything.*

The car door opened and Walter screamed.

Rowan jumped back. "Control yourself, Williams!"

"I'm sorry. It's just nerves."

Rowan closed the door and panted, wiping the water from his face. "I am at the proper age for a heart attack. You cannot do that to me."

"Manory, this is a horrible idea. We won't be able to see anything out there. I barely made it to the car."

"We can use the woods for shelter. The trees will make the rain bearable and shield us from the wind. We cannot wait. We have to hurry. You must trust me, my friend."

"What do you think happened to Bernice Lasciva?"

"We are going to find out."

They circled over the limestone and headed back onto the road. Walter drove past the first ten trees of the forest and pulled to the side. They scurried out of the car and into the wilderness.

From their vantage, the roof was still visible but the thickness of the forest prevented them from seeing any other part of the manor. Small waterfalls formed off the foliage and seeped into the muddy ground as their feet struggled to manage the terrain. Every twenty seconds a flash of lightning illuminated the interior of the forest, revealing a bullfrog or some other creature seeking shelter. The moon offered only faint shafts of light around the trees.

Walter yelled above the wind. "Did Daniels kill Tellum? Even if he did, he couldn't have killed Lasciva. He was with me. We would still be one killer short. Manory!"

Rowan did not seem to be listening. His feet kept planting and dislodging through the mud and his mind did the same with the possibilities.

*Tellum wrote the threat. He wrote chip chop, chip chop. Was he pretending to be Irene? He told me it was impossible. Why would he tell me that? Did Tellum and Daniels want Lasciva dead? Maybe they wanted to take over. Why write a threat? To make it look like someone was seeking vengeance for Irene and Dorothy? Why now? Twenty goddamn years later. Maybe Daniels double-crossed Tellum. And Bernice. Everyone here has met Bernice. Tellum picked her up. She is from Chicago. He picked up a German woman from Chicago. One coincidence too many is known as a scheme. What does it mean, Rowan? Who are Charles and Margaret? Why did they pretend to go to sleep? Ruth would never stick her gum under the table. Only a man would do that.*

The detective stepped into a hollow of liquid mud and toppled over. His arms blocked the fall, but his head snapped forward onto a log. The blood vessels in his nose burst and ripples of acute pain made their way along his face. His eyes became cloudy and his nose bled profusely. Walter squatted next to him. Lightning flashed and two wild green eyes reflected in front of them. They belonged to a bobcat regarding them without fear. The creature spewed a drowned-out hiss and took off into the night.

Walter lifted Rowan up and they wobbled on the drenched detritus. Rowan reached up to the bridge of his nose and cracked it sideways. A last giant spurt of blood shot down to his mouth but at least he was now able to breathe.

"Manory, let's go back. We're not going to make it out here."

"We continue."

They trudged to the back of the forest and came upon the embankment. The water had risen to a foot below capacity and crashed along the sides of the land in violent waves. Rowan took a large stick from the ground and chucked it into the current. The stick floated downstream, disappearing to the right, around the bend.

Walter continued to shout. "Where does it lead?"

Rowan pointed straight with his left hand. "The ridge continues to Fort Hill about twenty miles ahead." He held up his right hand and curved it. "This water leads to a cliff off the back of the ridge. I do not know how far." Rowan looked back toward the woods and noticed a desire path bearing toward the garden. "This is the easiest way to get to the creek from the back door. We will lie over there near the path and cover ourselves with branches. When he comes, we will see him dump the body."

"Who will we see dump the body?"

"Whomever."

"What if whomever sees us?"

"Whoever. Whoever will see us and we will see whomever. It is not a difficult concept to grasp, Williams."

"If you say so."

"If you do not move then we will not be seen."

Walter said, "Are you sure about this? We don't even know that

Bernice is dead."

"I am sure of nothing, my friend. Not anymore."

Rowan's blood stained smile was oddly comforting to Walter.

The detectives moved into the woods and lay flat on the ground. Rowan kept his eyes in the direction of the house and sopped up blood with his glove. Walter did his best not to look at the ground. He could feel tingling sensations all over his abdomen and imagined an army of bugs crawling under him, seeking entrance to his skin.

After two minutes, Walter moved inches from Rowan's ear and whispered. "Manory?"

"We must concentrate."

"I know, I know but… What could Tellum have been trying to say? It's a… It's a what? It had to be important. I suppose he could have been out of his mind at that point. Death probably has a way of clouding one's judgment."

Rowan kept looking forward.

"And Lasciva's brain. It was working just fine before his head was severed. They say the brain continues functioning for about thirty seconds. But how would they know? What kind of test would reveal that?"

In one reflexive movement, Rowan shifted his hand onto Walter's mouth. Walter's eyes, covered in rainwater, tilted forward.

A red raincoat shimmered in the scarcely available light as it advanced along the path through the forest. The hood hung loosely over the face by drooping corners. The only suspect Rowan could rule out was Willie. He was far too tall to be under that raincoat. Under the left arm, the shape carried a gunny sack made of burlap.

*That bag is not big enough for a body.*

Rowan watched exactly what he had anticipated. The figure's galoshes splashed in short strides and came to the edge of the embankment. With minimal strain, the sack was flung into the river.

Walter considered jumping the figure and wrestling him to the ground.

Rowan sensed his partner's unease and delicately touched him on the shoulder with his finger.

The raincoat-clad figure stood watching until the sack had been swallowed by the bend and then doubled back along the path. Rowan kept his finger on Walter's shoulder for a good minute as the mysterious figure faded into the trees toward the manor.

"What now?" asked Walter.

Rowan sprang up with the aid of Walter's shoulder and pulled him toward the embankment.

"The bag. There are overhanging trees all along the river. The water is high enough that a branch or even a stone might catch it. We have to go downriver and see if we can find it."

"Who was in the raincoat?"

"That was our man."

"Why didn't we follow him up the path? We could have taken him down."

"We know he threw a bag in the river. That means we know nothing. If we can find out what is in the bag, then perhaps we will know what has happened. Also, we have a missing gun to consider. I shall not make the same mistake twice. Come on."

They followed the river's path as it snaked to the back of the plateau. To their left, the forest continued, but the area behind the trees changed into mountainous terrain.

Upon reaching the back end of the ridge, Rowan felt a wave of excitement. "There!"

The sack dangled over the roaring water with its strap latched onto a low hovering branch at the edge of the cliff. The water flapped against the bottom of the sack before cascading down the precipice.

Rowan reached over the edge and a sudden burst of wind frightened his legs. "It is fruitless." He crouched next to the tree and held it tightly. "I will have to climb the tree and hang off the branch to get it. It is the only way." He planted a foot on the base of the trunk but Walter instinctively grabbed him.

"It'll break. It won't support you." He patted Rowan's stomach to demonstrate his lack of athleticism. "Is this bag vital to the case?"

"You know it is."

"Then this is how I make my rubes." Walter took off his gloves and found a footing in the gnarled bark. He hoisted himself up.

Rowan watched breathlessly as his partner grabbed hold of the branch with both hands and dangled himself over the water. "Be careful, Williams."

Walter moved one hand across the other until he was three feet from the sack. His weight bent the branch down and half of the burlap submerged. The strap loosened and it began swaying erratically. Walter kept his right hand on the branch and, with his back facing death, extended his left. His index and middle fingers stretched out in a desperate scissoring motion, trying to grasp some part of the sack. The tips of his fingers brushed against it and the slight contact emboldened him to stretch farther.

A panic overtook Rowan. He had a vision of himself alone on the ridge in the water logged gloom.

*Please, God. Do not take Williams, at least not yet.*

With a kick of the water, the sack popped up into Walter's clasped fingertips.

"Got it!"

For a fleeting second the mystery was solved.

Then Walter felt it slipping. He threw it into the air, attempting to catch it with a better grip. It fell against his dangling hand and he juggled it.

Rowan watched with dejection as the sack bounced off Walter's hand into the river and descended into Vicksburg.

Walter swung back along the branch and threw himself onto the ground.

"Are you all right, Williams?"

Walter held up his left hand and a sinuous stream of black cloth dangled from his fingers. It was one of Bernice Lasciva's arm-length gloves. Rowan grabbed the satin and twiddled it between his thumb and forefinger. Blood seeped from it and was quickly washed away by the rain.

Walter was apoplectic. "Her clothes! He dumped her clothes!"

Rowan stared into the abyss. "Maybe it was just her clothes, but I think something else may have been in there as well."

He was about to continue his thought when another gunny sack appeared, heading their way. It flowed unencumbered past them, avoided the branch, and disappeared over the edge.

Walter lifted himself off the ground. Without further comment, they walked back along the river. Walter's eyes alternated between the water and the forest while Rowan's focused on the ground.

"If you had to perform a discreet dismemberment in that house, where would you do it?" said Rowan.

Walter's face contorted.

"It was not really a question. I am thinking out loud, Williams. It helps me. Also, remember, you are going to say something that will inspire me."

"Don't hold your breath, Manory."

Rowan stopped and put his hand on Walter's shoulder. "You were incredibly brave back there, Walter. I do not know what I would do without you. This is especially true now. I am second-guessing every placement of the puzzle pieces. Failure has followed me from Chicago and I will not persevere alone."

"That's the nicest thing you've ever said to me." Walter felt a lightness in his chest that was quickly replaced by the shiver of gooseflesh over his body. "If we solve this case will you go back to being the old Manory?"

"I am positive."

"Fantastic. I'm good at making coffee, comforting widows, that kind of thing."

They returned to the path and knelt down among the trees. The water had risen past the edge of the grass and was now freely washing onto land like the tide of a beach.

Walter said, "Let's end this now. I'll move toward the house and wait. If he comes back to dump another sack, I'll follow him down the path. With this rain he won't hear me. I jump him from behind, you charge him from the front. There won't be any time for him to pull out a gun."

This haphazard plan was not Rowan's style. In an instant, anything could go wrong. As the rain steadily beat on his hood, he had a vision of Walter being shot like Agatha Brent and her child. He would not allow that to happen.

"All right, Williams, but I will be the one who waits near the manor. I want you to position yourself here. Do not move until I tackle him to the ground. Do you understand?"

"Manory?"

"What?"

Out came the schoolboy grin. "How much fun is this?"

Rowan shook his head with exasperation. "No movement until I take him down. Tell me you understand."

"I'm on the trolley, old man."

Rowan duck-walked up through the forest, snapping twigs and splashing in mud puddles until he found a satisfactory spot in the forest and positioned himself.

Minutes passed.

Spurred by the stress, his heartbeat sped to an unruly thudding and he grew faint.

*Not now. Please, not now.*

He closed his eyes and tried to remember Ling's parlor trick. Black ink surrounded his heart, the fat, pulsating myocardium slopping in it. The aerated ink drained from the chamber. All of his anxiety oozed out leaving a healthy, fulgent pink. A spinning top appeared on his heart. With his fingers he stopped the top and began twisting it in the opposite direction. As the imaginary toy gained speed, his pulse abated.

Rowan opened his eyes. The raincoat-clad man passed him down the path, carrying another sack, and the beating in his chest skipped all the speeds in between and settled back at racing. He was about to follow the mysterious figure toward Walter when…

*Oh, no.*

The rain dissipated and with the last bulbous drops, it ceased altogether. The surreal absence of rain amplified every sound. The thin howl of the wind, the rhythmic croaking of frogs, and the splat of drops from the trees seemed to reverberate.

The mystery man in the raincoat paused, and one of the black gloves reached into a pocket and pulled out Tellum's Colt Police Positive revolver. Rowan stared at the man's back, frozen by fear. Any movement could give him away. The moment seemed endless with murderer and detective so close together. Rowan could hear his pulse ricochet off the walls of his cochlear duct. He wondered if the man in the red raincoat could hear it as well.

The shape stood still for another moment and then finally walked out of sight.

*Please, Williams. Have the good sense not to do anything foolish.*

A thick drop landed on Rowan's coat and the rain began anew, mirroring his heart. It came like pellets, more furious than before. The calm between the storms had passed.

Rowan began to inch his way forward through the forest.

*Screw your courage to the sticking stone.*

A lightning bolt hit the ground in the distance. A gunshot quickly followed, and the detective jumped erect, losing his balance. He fell to the ground and cracked his nose on the exact same spot as before.

"Goddamnit!" he screamed, pressing his gloves against his face. "Williams!" He blindly struggled to his feet and spun around, unsure of where he was. A succession of lightning flashes followed, causing Rowan's blurred vision to go completely white. He bent down and closed his eyes tightly. He heard Walter's scream convert to thunder.

The detective slowly opened his eyes and saw the path in front of him. He slid along the mud until he came to Walter lying on his back. "Are you hit?"

"It was Daniels."

"Are you hit, Williams?"

Walter shook his head. "He missed. It was Daniels. I saw his face."

Rowan looked around the forest. "He must have run off. Williams,

I told you to wait for me. Do not ever put yourself at risk again. Do you hear me?"

Walter pointed toward the river and Rowan followed the direction of his finger. Near the embankment the opened burlap sack lay on a patch of muddy grass. The water tantalizingly danced around it, threatening to pull it into the river. Rowan dove and clutched the strap in his hand. He looked inside.

"Well," said Walter, "don't keep me in suspense."

Rowan's stomach churned. He turned the sack upside down and dumped the bloody contents in the mud.

Walter gagged. He swallowed and forced the words from his mouth. "Tell me we're close to the finish line."

"No, Williams. This is all wrong. It does not make sense."

"Why not?"

Rowan plucked one of the frayed and bloody feet from the ground and held it up to the moonlight. "From the look of it, I would have to conclude that this foot belonged to a man." He bent the toes. "Rigor has not set in either. I would say forty minutes at most."

"Is it Willie or Charles?"

"William is much too large for these to belong to him."

"Then it's Charles?"

"It is possible, but…"

"But what?"

Rowan pointed toward the top of the manor.

The flickering of candlelight swayed in Charles and Margaret's window.

# CHAPTER 12

# ROBBERY

Walter and Rowan emerged from the woods and passed the zinnia corollas in the garden. The thin, papery petals had surrendered their color to the soggy muck. They floated about the remains of Lasciva's once-beautiful garden like ashen lily pads.

Rowan stopped in front of the back door and squeezed his nose.

*Broken. God, I could use a cigarette.*

Walter yelled in his ear. "It makes you look tougher."

Rowan's brows snapped together.

"I'll call you Bruiser from now on, boss."

He cast a curious glance at Walter as the water dribbled off his hood and carried diluted blood into his mouth.

Walter gawped. "Did I do it?"

"Did you do what?"

"Did I inadvertently solve the case? You know, like you said. I'm going to say something irrelevant that will bust the thing wide open. Did I do it just now?"

"No."

"Then why did you look at me like that?"

"You have cheated death twice tonight. At the moment you are carrying a bag filled with gruesome dismemberment and yet your ebullience remains irrepressible and undimmed. The mystery of your childlike enthusiasm is unsolvable, even for me."

"I do my best."

Rowan turned to the door. "No talking when we are inside. We will head straight to the kitchen."

"What's in the kitchen?"

"Weapons."

The back door creaked open. On the oak surface, muddy footprints lay bathed by a muted rectangle of moonlight.

Rowan had not expected to hear anything, but the effect of the manor's silence was still jarring. Walter softly shut the door and eased the sack onto the floor. In the enveloping darkness, they shed their raincoats and galoshes, squeaked into the dining room, and went through the push doors to the kitchen.

Walter felt his way to the pantry and pulled out a large jar. He unscrewed the lid and had a whiff. "Pickled cherries."

Rowan took a box of matches from the carving table and lit a candle.

The light revealed Walter dangling a cherry over his mouth. "Don't judge me. I know it isn't professional but I'm absolutely famished." He dropped it and offered the jar to Rowan.

He refused with a raise of his hand. "What happened out there, Williams?"

Walter spat a pit into the trash and shook the water from his hair. He spoke in the monotone of remembrance. "When the rain stopped, I panicked. It's hard to explain. I had forgotten what the world sounded like without rain. Suddenly, I could hear everything. It was unnerving to say the least. Then, I saw the red raincoat coming down the path. I waited for you to appear behind it, but you didn't come."

"For this, I offer you my sincerest apologies. I was just as flummoxed by the rain as you were." He extended his index finger. "However, I distinctly remember my orders."

"I'll stop you right there. Your orders were followed. I didn't move."

"Noted. Continue."

"After he got close to the embankment, the rain began again, stronger this time. When the lightning struck, he must have seen me. He fired the gun and I hit the deck. It was chaos. Everything happened so quickly. I looked up and he was gone. Then the lightning flashed again and again, maybe four times in a row."

"Yes, I remember."

"That's when I saw his face. He had moved out farther into the forest, but he turned around and I saw him."

"And you are certain it was Daniels?"

"I couldn't see very well, but I'm sure it was him."

Rowan bent his head. "It makes things more difficult if it was Daniels."

Walter struggled to describe the sight of Paul Daniels near the river. "His face had this look of shock and disorientation. It was as if he couldn't believe he had been caught. He looked terrified, inhumanly so. Just thinking of it gives me chills. It was him."

Rowan was quiet for a few minutes. He replayed the night's events in his mind and tried to find the connective threads. He ran his tongue across the small crack in the back of his molar.

*This case has already turned bloodier than I could have possibly imagined. Have I made some blunder, some monumental gaffe that will make the Tommy Brent case pale by comparison? Is Pyrrhic victory the best I can hope for?*

He snapped out of his daze. "Right. Okay. We have to check on

Charles. Let us hope he is dead."

"That's a bit rough. He doesn't seem like that bad of a chap to me."

"No, Williams. If the body parts in that bag are not Charles's body parts and they are not Willie's body parts and they are not Lasciva's body parts and they are not Tellum's body parts and they are not a woman's body parts, and Daniels carried them out, so they are not his body parts then…" Rowan held his hands out with his palms up.

"Then that would be bad."

"Because?"

"Because that would mean that there is… or rather there was someone on this ridge that we were not aware of. Someone we'll never have the pleasure of meeting."

"Precisely." Rowan reached to pull a knife from the block. The top slot, reserved for the butcher's knife, was vacant. "It seems someone has already taken one of the knives." He selected a utility knife and pressed the tip against his index finger. "This should be suitable enough."

Walter stared at the blade and spoke haltingly, the cherries affecting his pronunciation. "Manory, there's something I've been meaning to ask you, something that's been on my mind."

"Williams, my nose is broken. Have pity on me."

"I was just wondering if you wouldn't mind telling me—"

"If you make me laugh, I will stab you."

"You didn't kill them, did you?"

Rowan giggled painfully. "Oh, God."

Walter drank some cherry juice and slid out a knife for himself. "Just so I know, which case are we working on now? Is it the Lasciva case or the Roberts case?"

"I will tell you when I have decided."

Walter nodded. "Upstairs?"

As they ascended the spiral staircase, the candlelight elongated their wavering shadows. The detectives trod lightly on the steps, but the slower and gentler their footsteps, the louder the wood seemed to creak.

Rowan stood in front of the sliver of light under Charles's door. "Ready, Williams?" he whispered.

Walter knocked. "Margaret. It's Walter and Rowan. We'd like to talk to you and Charles, if he's still with us."

No answer came.

Rowan stepped in front of his partner. "Please disregard what I said earlier. It is essential that you open the door." He waited another moment and then grabbed the knob, twisting it in tiny increments. The door opened freely.

Several candles burned on the nightstand of the empty room and the rain's shadows dripped along the walls.

"It looks like nobody is home." Walter opened the closet. "Their suitcases are still here." He looked under the bed. "Nothing."

Rowan lit the six candles in the wall mounts of the hall. He looked around at the three other bedroom doors in wide-eyed wonder. "I do not believe this." He shouted, "Hello!"

No one answered.

Rowan banged the butt end of the knife against his thigh. "No, no, no." He ran to every door and opened them one by one. Each room was vacant. "I gave very clear instructions, easily understandable."

Walter scratched his head with his blade. "This feels like an awful joke. Where could they be?"

From downstairs, the sound of rain amplified and then was muted with a slam.

Rowan whispered, "It's the front door."

Heavy footsteps trod across the downstairs hallway.

Rowan clutched at Walter's collar and pulled him into Charles's room. "We have been given a second chance. When he comes upstairs, you tackle him and hold his arms. I will put my knife to his throat."

The stairs produced their familiar chirr until finally, the sound of two thudding feet landed on the upstairs floor.

The detectives crouched, ready to leap forward. A large shadow spread across the hallway and passed the door. It stopped.

"Anybody here?"

Rowan charged out from the room and pointed the knife. "Goddamnit, Aikes, what did I tell you? I said to stay in your room."

Willie defensively held up his hands. "Relax, it's only me." He dropped his hands and leaned forward. "Good God, what happened to your face?"

Rowan ignored the question. "It is impossible for me to do my job when everyone is lying to me and no one does as they are told."

"Mr. Manory—"

"I am waiting, William."

Willie struggled to come out with it. "Mr. Manory, something strange is happening in this manor."

Rowan's eyes grew. "Really? Is that a fact? Did you realize this, Williams?"

Walter said, "I must have overlooked it."

Rowan said, "Well, we are certainly glad you are here to inform us, otherwise we would have no idea. We thought this was a usual Friday night in Mississippi."

Willie Aikes blurted out, "Mr. Lasciva…"

The knife dropped to Rowan's side. "What about him?"

"He's been robbed."

Rowan took a long pause. "Did he have a safe hidden

somewhere?"

"It weren't money he was robbed of."

"Show me."

Rowan and Walter followed Willie down the steps and into the office, each holding a lit candle. Robert Lasciva's body and head lay unprotected on the floor. The armor and the ax were gone. The body was clothed with his Livingston suit and Brooks shoes. The head faced up with its eyes open.

Walter looked under the desk and in the closet before collapsing onto the crimson sofa. "I feel like we were further ahead the last time we were in this room. Where is the armor, Manory?"

"I believe the location of the ax is far more important right now."

Willie remained next to the splintered door frame. "I was having a nightmare and a loud noise from outside woke me up. That's why I left my room. I knocked on all the doors, but everybody was gone. Being all by myself, I got scared and ran down here to check."

Rowan drifted around the room and finally stopped at Lasciva's desk. He found a small pouch of tobacco in the top drawer and rolled a cigarette. "You found him like this?"

"Aye. I thought maybe… I don't know what the hell I thought." Willie wiped his forehead with a handkerchief. "I went out the front door and I saw that Charles's car was gone. Then I walked around the estate. I didn't see nobody out there."

Rowan dragged smoke through his throat in a long sustained breath. "Was it a gunshot?"

"Huh?"

"The noise that woke you up, was it a gunshot?"

"Coulda been. Hey, can I get one of those, Mr. Manory?"

He handed Aikes the lit cigarette. "What were you dreaming about, Willie?"

"My brother. He's got a cherry tree in his backyard and I dreamed it attacked me. It sounds silly now, but when I woke up, I remembered every detail. I never remember my dreams. They say that if you have a vivid dream it must be something important. Where is everybody? Did you find Bernice?"

Rowan held his head in his hands and flared his nostrils. "I have nightmares all the time, William."

"What are yours about?"

"Agatha."

"Who is Agatha?"

The detective had dreamt of Agatha at least once a week since that day in March.

Walter could not bear the silence any longer. "What now, boss? We can't go home."

"Come." Rowan knelt beside the cadaver and Walter joined him on the opposite side. "Put him on his backside."

They flipped Lasciva's stiffened, headless body on its back. The repulsive thudding sound of its contact with the floor made Walter flinch.

"Should we really be touching him like this?"

Rowan said, "This is an unusual circumstance, Williams. It calls for some unusual actions. I would love nothing more than to make a telephone call and have a professional look at the body and collect fingerprints." He poked his finger through a tear in Lasciva's suit coat. "What have we here?

Walter found one on the shoulder. "There's another one. There are more on the legs as well. They're all over."

Rowan lifted the shirt off the body. Tiny pricks in the flesh matched the tears of the shirt and a large scar crossed the chest. "The skin is punctured but there is no blood so it must have been done after he was killed. It appears the armor was removed with a crowbar. I imagine it is very difficult to remove armor from a recently dead body. In Frederick's time they would wait until a day had passed and the process of rigor mortis had reversed."

"Who is Frederick?" asked Willie.

Irritation crept into Rowan's brain. He quickly sought to quell it.

*A little more Williams, a little less Manory.*

"You see, William, I believe the armor belonged to Frederick the

Victorious which would explain its high price tag."

Walter pointed to Lasciva's chest. "How do you think he got that scar?"

"It is an old wound. It looks consistent with a knife fight."

Rowan reached into the suit coat and found nothing until he came to the inner slit pocket on the right. He pulled out a folded sheet of paper. Rowan walked to the desk and laid it down.

He read it aloud.

"Alas, detective, the night is over and the dawn has revealed two more missing members of the party, just as I had promised. Perhaps you need a helping hand. This is your second and final note. Look at it carefully, it will provide a clue. Chip chop, chip chop."

"Did Tellum write that one too?"

"Yes. He was an awfully busy man before he died."

Walter tried to close Lasciva's eyelids, but they would not budge and the pale head continued to stare. A red strip had developed across the irises and lent them an eerie chatoyant gleam from the candlelight. "Remember how I was lost before?"

"Yes?"

"Well now I'm adrift."

"The deceased Tellum seems to have abandoned his rhyming taunt," said Rowan. "His sense of timing, however, remains defective.

Obviously we were meant to discover this note tomorrow morning."

"According to the notes, there should be a total of four dead. We have Tellum, Lasciva, possibly Bernice and then who? Charles?"

Willie shook his head. "I told you. The Fiat is gone."

As his desperation mounted, Rowan felt his throat constrict. The bags under his bloodshot eyes gained weight.

*This is the time to push forward. When all seems lost, you will make your greatest strides.*

The detective forced a look of optimism onto his face. "We have a clue. The note tells us so."

Walter chuckled. "I don't think Willie and I are as adept as you. What clue does this note provide?"

"I already told you."

"Maybe I wasn't listening. Run it by me one more time."

"The third note does not rhyme. This must be the clue. It is a major difference between the three."

"We were supposed to find it in the morning, as you said. Why do you think it was planted on Lasciva's body now? It's premature. Did Tellum know that he was one of the four? If the armor hadn't been removed, we wouldn't even have found the blasted thing."

"It may have been planted on him earlier tonight, before he got into the armor." Rowan looked at Willie furtively. "Does this clue mean anything to you?"

"I don't write poetry."

Rowan and Walter shot each other a glance and in unison said, "The library."


The massive wall of books dwarfed Rowan's body as he stood before it. The muscles in his legs grappled with their encasing skin like enraged animals in a sack. He did his best to concentrate, using the blade of the knife to track the titles. "Lock the door, Williams."

Walter removed the key from the latch and did as he was instructed. "We have to remember to blow out the candles from upstairs. Ruth said they could start a fire."

"I can do it," said Willie.

Rowan continued reading the titles. "I think you should have a seat, Mr. Aikes."

"I might as well be useful to you."

Rowan turned. "No one is going to leave my sight again. Sit down, William."

Willie shrugged and lumbered to the farthest sofa. "I just wanted to help. If that's how you feel about it, I won't offer no more."

"You can help just fine by sitting there and talking to me. Tell me William—"

"For the last time, my name is Willie."

"Is there a poetry section?"

"What?"

"I am speaking English. Is there a specific section designated for a collection of poetry?"

Willie's eyebrows went limp and his collarbones hunched inward as if expecting a blow. "I can't read."

Rowan looked down and saw his reflection in the knife. He slipped it into his pocket. "It is of no importance."

Walter hunched down and looked at the lower shelves in the corner. "Here we are. Uhhh…Byron, Thoreau, Whitman, Poe. What are we looking for?"

"I am not sure. Where would you hide a clue?"

Walter flipped through the collection of Poe. "Well, if the lack of rhyme is what we're after, wouldn't we avoid the poetry section?"

"Perhaps we are meant to look at free verse." Rowan pulled out the Whitman book and riffled the pages.

"Manory, there are too many books here. We could spend days looking through them."

Rowan placed the footstool against the right corner of the wall and checked the titles. "The clue was not meant to be solved over such a long period of time."

"Why would someone write clues anyway? It seems counterintuitive, doesn't it?"

"There are many reasons to write clues, but I do not wish to contemplate them now."

Walter glanced over at Rowan. "What are you looking for?"

"A reference book is often used as a rhyming aid. There must be something to help us with our cadence." He came to a large tome in the upper right corner. His eyes lit up. "Eureka. *Manipulus Vocabulorum*. If one needs to write a poem or a song or perhaps a harbinger of doom, this would be the book of choice." He placed his index finger on the spine. "Fingers crossed, Williams."

He tilted the book off the shelf and a clicking noise came from the opposite end. The left side of the wall jutted forward a few inches.

A sense of childlike wonder overcame the three men. It was reminiscent of adventure stories of pirates finding buried treasure.

Upon removing the book completely, a lever became visible at the back of the shelf. Rowan hopped off the stool. "Go ahead, Williams."

Walter pulled open the last section of shelves, exposing a gray, stone passage.

Rowan stuck in a candle, followed by his head.

"Here's your secret passage, old man. Too bad it's on the wrong side of the house."

Rowan reached to the left and ran his hand down a smooth stone wall. Sickly wet condensation trickled down and settled on a gravelly floor, creating muddy sand. "Even worse, it does not appear to lead anywhere."

"It's sealed? Doesn't that defeat the purpose of a passage?"

The detective looked to the right. "Now I understand."

"What is it?"

Rowan handed Walter the candle, threw his suit coat on the floor and rolled up his sleeves. "It is not sealed. It appears this passage goes to the right. I would guess that it makes a hairpin curve and heads to the back of the manor."

"Like a 'u.'"

"More like a 'j' but yes. Unfortunately, this means there is a partition between the passage and this doorway. We will not remain in visual contact."

Walter shook his head. "See, that won't matter because we're both going inside."

"Unacceptable. If we both enter the passage, it will be easy to trap us by shutting this door. I need you to stay here."

"Manory—"

"Besides, someone has to keep an eye on our friend."

Willie threw up his hands in frustration. "No one needs to keep an eye on me. I'll go through the damned passage if you want me to."

Rowan ignored him. "If I run into any trouble, I will call out to you. Do not leave this room, Williams." He took back the candle and disappeared inside.

Walter leaned into the passage. The tiny shimmer from Rowan's candle moved along the inky black space and vanished around the corner.

Rowan yelled back. "It is completely dark. I can only see a few feet in front of me. I must go slowly."

"Be careful, old man." Walter turned back to Willie. "Sorry about all this. It's not that we don't trust you. It's that we can't afford to."

Willie puckered his lips. "Maybe I can't trust *you*. No one turned up dead here until you fellas came. You ever think of that?"

"Willie, if your brother is here—"

"My brother is at home, wondering where the hell I am."

"I know, but if he's here, I think you should say so now. It'll save us a lot of trouble."

"He ain't here."

"It's just that if he *is* here—"

"He ain't here!"

"But if he *is*..."

"What? What if he's here?"

"Well, if he is, I think some of him might be in a bag in the kitchen."

202

Willie looked incredulous. "You're out of your goddamned mind."

"This kind of work will do that to you." Walter stuck his head back in the passage.

"Manory, are you okay?"

Silence.

"Manory!"

"What?"

"Are you all right?"

"Yes, I just…"

"What?"

"I just have yet to begin."

# CHAPTER 13

# IN THE DARK

Hallucinatory swirls of light formed in the black and danced deep into the passage. Rowan closed his eyes in an effort to will them away. He could taste the air. Stale and frowzy, it audibly scraped down his windpipe and settled like heavy sand. His aching lungs rasped as they sifted scant traces of oxygen. The roof of his mouth went dry and he tried to wet it, but his tongue stuck like damp clothes on skin. He opened his eyes.

The flame, so timid and fragile, struggled in defiance of the black maw. It offered sallow murmurs of light to combat the strangling, charcoal-etched space. At the farthest point of illumination, the images turned indistinct like an oil painting, suggesting rather than showing and finally fading into utter black.

He moved the candle next to the stone side of the passage. At various points the wall took the shape of a bubbled caul, but it showed no cracks or markings of any kind. The wet gray glistened with illusory movement. The fire began wobbling at the wick from the intensity of his breath. He raised the candle high.

*Is this where Irene is buried? The light of my courage shall not be swayed by the shadows surrounding me.*

Rowan turned his right ear forward and listened to the refrigerated echo of silence. The whole world could have been gone.

The gravel crackled under his shoe with his first step.

"If anyone is in here, I recommend you reveal yourself." His voice carried an authoritarian tenor but even he could recognize the undertone of trailing fear.

The candlelight inched forward with his movement, leaving more blackness behind him to go along with the seemingly endless amount in front.

"Mr. Daniels? Are you here?"

*The best swimmers drown. Perhaps this is your tomb.*

He clenched the knife tighter and held it trembling in front of him.

The tip of the candle made contact with a cobweb and it erupted in a brief burst of flame. Rowan gasped as a shape on the floor outlined on his retina.

*What was that? I saw it. Something. I do not know what.*

Walter's disembodied voice called out like a ghost. "What was that?"

Rowan clutched at his chest. "Nothing. It was—"

"What did you say?"

"I said it was nothing!"

Rowan fidgeted with the remains of cobweb in his hair and dropped the knife. It pinged and rattled on the gravel. "Christ!" Panic stirred.

"This is your last warning, Mr. Daniels. Come forward. We are not leaving this ridge for a few days, so we may as well make the best of our situation. There is no need for more senseless murder."

His voice faded down the passage into nothingness. He retrieved the knife from the floor and looked back toward the library. Where was it? How far had he walked?

*Am I gone from reality? Is this really happening or is it just another episode?*

With panting breath and a quickening heartbeat, he yelled out. "Is everything okay, Williams?"

No answer came.

"Williams."

Again.

"Walter!"

"What is it, Manory? Did you find Bernice?"

Rowan breathed easier and let out a nervous laugh. "Not yet. I just wanted to make sure you were still with me."

"No worries, old man. I'm here. Shall I come in?"

"No. Stay with Willie."

Rowan stared at the spot ten feet ahead where he had seen the shape. He tried to reconstruct it.

*If zis house is searched, vat vill zey find? I vonder.*

He moved forward at the same pace as before until a familiar odor hit his nostrils. It was the triggering vestigial scent of copper. The vibrating light shimmering on the moisture of the walls turned from gray to a membranous red. The stone began to pulse in and out as he circled within the corridor. The walls were covered in blood. A piercing trill rang out from the tip of his shoe and Rowan lowered the candle.

The object lay in a soupy mixture of blood and gravel.

Rowan called out to Walter. "I have located the ax!"

"Is the armor there too?"

"No. They did not go together anyway. Williams, do you—"

A shaft of light at the back end of the passage stalled Rowan's question. He blew out the candle. A shadow entered the far end and closed the entrance, returning the passage to black.

Rowan knelt and silently placed the extinguished candle on the floor. His arm extended forward with the knife and he stood up.

Two separate plops came from the ground.

*Galoshes.*

"Do I what?" asked Walter.

*Shut up, Williams.*

The revolver's hammer clicked ever so faintly. It was followed by slow, steady, scraping steps forward.

Rowan dared not speak. His feet moved in reverse. The gravelly sound on the floor seemed to echo a thousand times louder than before as the thumping in his chest began once again. The now invisible walls closed in and his diaphanous hold on reality let go completely. He collapsed backward. Paralyzing pain in his chest choked the air from his throat. He lay helpless and alone in the tenebrous space, his limbs turtle-like and flailing.

*No.*

Rowan's arm slammed against the stone wall and his back slid along the floor, moving the gravel bits against one another. The sounds slowly dissipated and entered his ear as the same homogenous hum.

A foot bumped into his leg and with his twitching left arm, he felt the ax brush up against him as it was being lifted off the ground.

*This is my tomb.*

The detective tried to make out the face of his soon-to-be killer, but saw only phosphenes in the dark. They began as small strips but grew in thickness and shot forward toward the killer.

He managed one last, breathless word. "Irene."

Images from his life appeared in panorama. He fell from the tree and along with the pain of a broken arm he felt the guilt of childhood. Terror enveloped him as he watched his father strike his mother. His dog lay dying in the street and he desperately wanted the animal to fathom the depths of his sorrow. Agatha Brent slumped back on her couch. He somehow saw every hair of the fly landing on her body. Even the unearthly awareness of this life review could not decipher the emotions of that event, so deeply had Rowan suppressed them.

The images in his head went black. For a long time, there was nothing.

*Is this death?*

A quivering pocket of breath ripped from Rowan's chest. He inhaled and the horrible scent came again.

*It is not. I am still tucked away in a narrow passage on a ridge in the middle of a storm. Thank God.*

A tiny flicker of light appeared above him and became more and more intense until he made out the shape of Walter's face.

"Manory, what happened?"

Rowan's voice sputtered. "The killer…"

"Steady, old man. Wait here."

Walter ran to the end of the passage. Rowan tried to stop him, but his arms disobeyed. He was left alone again in the darkness.

A familiar thud came from behind him. Two giant hands tucked under his arms and lifted him. The musk of Willie Aikes was instantly recognizable through the copper.

"Come on, detective. Let's get you back to the library."

Rowan leaned on Willie as his heels dragged along the gravel. He was pulled around the bend and temporarily blinded from the light of the library.

"Thank you, Willie."

"Hey, you got my name right."

Willie lowered Rowan onto the sofa. "Just take it easy now. I'll get you a drink."

"No panther piss, please."

Willie unlocked the door and ran to the kitchen.

Walter came in, soaking, with knife in hand. He rushed to Manory's side. "It was Daniels, wasn't it?"

"I could not see him. Where does the passage lead?"

"The dining room."

"I knew that cabinet was abnormally thick."

"Yeah, the side springs open. He ran out the back door. I tried to find him but he must have run into the woods."

Willie brought a glass of water and handed it to Rowan. He chugged it. "Williams, was there anything else in the passage?"

"As a matter of fact, there was. I don't know quite what to make of it but there were shelves at the back. They had lots of raincoats, several pairs of galoshes, and this." Walter held out a tiny cylindrical case.

Rowan flexed his legs and forced himself off the sofa. He paced gingerly around the room.

Blood had tracked all through the library. Splotchy red patches covered the sofas.

*The longer this weekend at Lasciva Manor, the more it resembles some hellish puzzle with no interlocking edges. Salvation has become perdition and it is perfect hell. The ill-timed clues, the lack of resources, the ungodly weather, and my failing body are all conspiring against me. How long until I crack under the strain?*

Willie, Rowan, and Walter stood in front of the phonograph. The detective opened the canister and stuck two fingers inside of the wax cylinder. He placed it on the mandrel and turned the hand crank.

An audible, empty hiss played through the pavillon, but it was quickly taken over by a susurrous moaning. The unearthly sound then morphed into a painful screech like nails being dragged over rock. Rowan quickened the pace as screaming sounds took over. For three minutes it continued until finally the original empty hiss played out and the cylinder came to its end.

"I hope to God that isn't the new craze in music," said Williams.

"What did that sound like to you, Willie?" asked Rowan.

Willie said, "Like ghosts."

"That is exactly what it sounded like."

Two beams of light rolled through the French windows and came to a halt. The Fiat settled along the drive and the lights shut off.

Rowan tensed his muscles so hard that they shook.

Walter said, "Another episode?"

"Marauding little worm." He grabbed Walter's knife from the table.

"Manory?"

Suddenly galvanized into action, Rowan ran outside into the rain. The car doors opened. Charles and Margaret stepped out.

Charles said, "Mr. Manory, what happened to you?"

"Gone for a joy ride?"

"Charles!" screamed Margaret.

The detective held the knife to Charles's side and his barely controlled rage showed in his hoarse, unforgiving voice. "I am no longer responsible for your safety."

Walter rushed out the door. "Manory, old man. Relax. It's okay."

Charles said, "I'm sorry, I don't follow. We haven't done anything."

"I told you to stay in your room."

"We needed to make sure the bridge was truly disabled," said Margaret. She turned to Willie. "My apologies, Mr. Aikes, but trust is not something that comes easily after what we have witnessed tonight."

Rowan's head bobbed. "You said it, lady."

"Shall we go inside and discuss it like adults? I for one don't want to stand here in the rain and—"

The sound of a gunshot rang out in the night, causing Rowan to jump back. Two more came in quick succession. They all looked toward the manor.

"It came from the river," said Willie.

"Where's Ruth?" asked Charles.

"Everyone inside. We will cut through the manor and go out the back door." Rowan pointed a nicotine-stained fingernail toward Margaret. "No more games."

# CHAPTER 14

# FIRE AND RAIN

*Bernice Lasciva... Robert had a history with you. Jack drove you from Ashland. Daniels knew you. Willie and Ruth despised you. Where did you go? Walter saw Daniels at the river. Whose body was in the bag? There is only one possibility and it is not possible. I have done everything correctly.*

The party cut through the manor and wallowed into what was left of the garden. The weight of their saturated clothes pulled down like an extra dose of gravity. All about them, the trees bent and moaned as the gale whipped the rain into their eyes.

Rowan pointed and screamed above the wind. "Willie and Charles, cut through the right side of the forest." He pulled Walter and Margaret close. "Go straight through the path and wait at the river. I will go through the left side." He held out his hands and brought them together. "We meet at the center."

The partygoers scattered helter-skelter. In between the thunder, a distant sound of dislodging rock joined the general turmoil.

As Rowan neared the obliterated demarcation of land and creek, Ruth's desperate and directionless gurgled cries became detectable. He passed the last tree and debris hurled past his head, forcing him to his knees.

*Focus, Rowan. Where is she?*

He scanned the river bit by bit trying to distinguish hallucination from truth.

*There.*

Ruth was desperately clutching a tree branch. There was a splatter of blood across her arm. The top of her lace slip stuck to her shoulders. The rapids slammed against her head, rendering her body as limp as a ragdoll.

Rowan ran toward the embankment and his entirety immediately plunged under the water. In the murk, his body flipped while moving forward at rapid speed. Left utterly prostrate, his tired limbs fought against the superior tide as he flowed downstream in pounding spurts.

He felt a tug against his collar followed by a tight snap at his neck. Ruth had grabbed him with her free arm. The bullet wound along her bicep flared, causing her to screech. The fabric of his shirt ripped and he clutched at her body. She grabbed the mealy bark with both hands as Rowan wrapped his arms around her torso.

The other four spotted them from the pathway to the river. They got as close as they could and formed a chain of bodies. Williams stood at the end. He pulled Ruth's good arm, and the group kinetically lifted the imperiled out of the water and onto the sludge.

Walter draped his sodden suit coat over Ruth as she coughed up ingested rainwater.

She looked up at him with red-rimmed eyes. "It was Daniels. Daniels."

"We know. Let's get you inside."

Rowan's head rose from the mud. He eyed the manor between the foliage. Resplendent golden flames danced in front of an upstairs window.

*We forgot to blow out the candles.*

He began to wordlessly mouth instructions when the first monolithic boulder leavened the density of the trees, its crash mocking the thunder in the sky and leaving everyone in stunned disarray. Muddy water engulfed the entire forest. Rowan bobbed like the coffins. His ears alternated between the subaqueous, deafening silence and the chaos of the known world. There was no control. His awareness slackened and then was swallowed whole by circumstance. The slight connection to the here and now vanished completely. He was gone.

The aridity of the room covered him like a mother's blanket. Rowan spread his arms wide to garner as much of the warmth as possible. He lit an inevitable cigarette and felt the smoke curl along his tongue before entering his throat. It came out of his mouth in rolling billows.

The tawny clay of the walls and ceiling seemed to bake in the heat. The structure could have been made that very morning or thousands of years ago. His eyes drifted along the cracks in the wall before settling on Robert Lasciva at the head of the table.

The sound of flowing water began as a quiet murmur, but soon became a rushing noise.

Lasciva stood and held up a glass. He screamed over the pounding waves. "A toast to the world's finest detective."

Agatha stood next to him, gently rocking her dead baby. "Manory couldn't help us either."

Then they were all there, standing up and toasting him behind a table that stretched to infinity.

Jack Tellum coughed and took a swig from his flask. "Yeah, well, this will put some hair on your liver."

Daniels giggled. "I think he needs his mommy, the poor dear."

Rowan puffed on his cigarette.

*"There must be an explanation."*

Margaret raised Charles's right hand and waved it like a marionette. Charles's mouth moved, but her voice came out. "Fancy a game of cricket?"

*"Where is Williams?"*

Ruth leaned close to Rowan and he felt her breath on his ear. "You and I have a lot in common, Mr. Manory. I can help you solve this case if you just listen to me. Everything happens for a reason."

He swallowed.

*"Williams?"*

Willie spread out his arms. "You keep calling people by their wrong name. Don't ask me who. I just work here. Have you seen my brother?"

Rowan tried to run but he felt the force of a crowd of people pouncing on his back. He fell to his knees as the noise of the rushing water faded and was replaced by the horrible scratching moans from the cylinder.

Daniels pulled Rowan's thin hair and directed his head toward an empty chair. "Now watch, Manory. Watch very carefully."

Walter appeared from the corner of Rowan's vision and sat at the chair.

*"Williams."*

A spider monkey leapt onto Walter's head and raised an ax high into the air.

Rowan stopped breathing. The scratching ceased and a dead silence took over.

Walter grinned. "You know, in Morocco, they train monkeys to do just about anything."

The ax came down and tore into Walter's neck. Again and again the monkey swung as arterial blood spurted indiscriminately about the room. Finally, Walter's body fell forward and the head rolled under the table. The monkey leapt off the chair to fetch it.

Daniels whispered in Rowan's ear. "Do you see?"

*"See what?"*

The monkey crawled to Rowan and held Walter's head to the side. The mouth and eyes were wide open.

*"Do I see what?"*

The monkey slowly moved Walter's head in front of its own.

Walter's head said, "It's just a parlor trick, Manory."

The invisible crazed mob let go of Rowan and he stumbled to his feet. The partygoers pointed at him and jeered. The detective stood, scarlet with mortification. He puffed at the completed cigarette and held out his hands as the building and his body vanished. Only his hands remained, floating in total black.

The noise of water returned.

One drop fell.

Another.

Soon the rain began in earnest.

-------------------------------------------------------------------------------

A slap woke Rowan from his turbulent slumber. His hearing turned up as if someone had twisted a radio's knob.

"It's a landslide! Get up, old man! We have to move now!"

When Rowan put his feet on the ground, the waist-high water quickly pulled them out from under him. Walter waded toward the front lawn, dragging Rowan behind him. The top of the manor blazed uncontrollably and lit the starless sky with burnt amber. The back door of the Fiat swung open and Rowan dove onto the seat next to an unconscious Ruth. Walter squeezed beside him and shut the door. Aikes, Charles, and Margaret sat squished together in the front seat.

The car buckled and lifted a few feet as water burst through the front door of the manor and knocked it loose from its hinges. The Fiat drifted toward the edge of the plateau. Everyone braced themselves for the plunge.

It never came.

The rush finally abated and the car settled as the last push of water crossed out into the valley and drained off. Rowan dreamily looked over his shoulder. A section of the manor's roof collapsed and steam erupted from the meeting of fire and water. He leaned toward slumber and told himself a delirious bedtime prayer.

*Now I lay me down to sleep. I pray the Lord my soul to keep. If I should be decapitated before I wake, I pray the Lord my soul to take.*

# CHAPTER 15

# VOICED AND UNVOICED CONSONANTS

Manory awoke to the snoring of Willie Aikes and a rank odor. His neck snapped forward with a painful jolt. A slight mist dribbled through the gray murk of the foggy Mississippi dawn and the barest glimpse of the sun appeared through a hole in the clouds.

He peeled his lips apart and spoke hoarsely. "Williams, wake up."

Walter started speaking before he realized where he was. "Five more minutes, Mom."

They stumbled out of the car and stretched their wilted muscles. All across the estate, uprooted willow trees lay next to ripped patches of sod. The top of the manor continued to steam from the eve's fire.

Walter said, "This is what war must look like. It's probably what it feels like as well."

"How did we survive?" asked Rowan.

Walter scratched his belly and yawned. "It's a miracle, old man. When the tidal wave carried you off, I was sure you were headed straight into the valley. But I found you."

"Thank you, my friend."

"I bet you're glad I insisted on tagging along."

"Yes, of course."

The flooded valley below was swaddled by rolling billows of fog. Walter peered over the edge. "Do you think Daniels made it?"

Rowan shook his head.

"What makes you so sure? If we all made it, he could have."

"No, Williams. Mr. Daniels is now part of the Vicksburg landscape one way or another."

Walter looked over the remaining suspects in the Fiat. "Now that you've had a chance to sleep on it, have you any idea what happened? Does it even matter now?"

Rowan sat on the wet ground and made a steeple of his fingers. "I know some pieces of the puzzle but the unitary photograph is beyond me."

"I'm sure with a bit more time—"

"No, Williams. We have a sunken crime scene. I fear that no evidence will solve this mystery." He rubbed his temples.

Walter put an invisible cigarette into the corner of his mouth. "Let us go over what we know so far."

"The first murder is easy enough to solve. Daniels killed Tellum."

"Pretend I'm stupid."

"Every year I attend the APC conference in Chicago. Last year's meeting featured a speech about antifreeze. It used to be made with methanol. Two years ago, it was announced that a new process had been developed. Antifreeze would now be made using ethylene glycol. It is an organic compound used to make dynamite. Drinking it would cause the symptoms that Tellum experienced. It is also odorless and its only featured taste is sweetness. As Margaret told you, the panther piss was very sweet."

"But Daniels also drank the piss."

"Of course it is recommended that you visit a doctor in cases of ethylene glycol poisoning. However, in a pinch one may need only to drink alcohol. Daniels drank more than enough to offset a small sip of piss. According to Charles, Daniels immediately drank three full glasses. He was probably scared out of his mind. Lots of bravery was on display last night."

"Did you know he killed Tellum the moment I told you about the antifreeze in his car?"

"Of course I did. Southerners do not use antifreeze. They have no need for it. Water will do the trick."

"Why did he kill Tellum? They were friends."

Rowan shook his head. "Maybe he was worried that Tellum was getting closer to Lasciva. Daniels might have thought he was being cheated of profits. Perhaps he was jealous. Who knows?"

"But in the will…"

Rowan laughed. "I will need the assistance of a probate official to be sure, but I am quite certain it is a forgery."

"I see." Walter shrugged. "Manory, there's something I've been meaning to ask you."

"I am so happy you are here to cheer me up on this godforsaken morning."

"No, it's a serious question. Why did you get so angry at Charles? I thought you were going to kill him. I've never seen you lose it like that."

"Everyone lies. Usually I have the resources to deal with lies but not here. If he had simply told me the truth, I would have had less to deal with and less to think about. Also, my body is betraying me and I am not even forty years old. It is frustrating."

Walter thought it through. "He's not Robert's nephew, is he?"

"He is not Robert's nephew and he is not British. Lasciva showed me a photo of a young Charles holding a cricket bat. The boy in the photo is left-handed. Charles, or whatever his name is, signed the paper with his right hand. I had noticed him shaking with his right hand earlier in the evening, but many left-handed people do this out of habit because right-handed people make up ninety percent of the population. That is why I had him sign his name."

"And how do you know he's not British?"

"He sounds like a high school production of Shakespeare, he mispronounced Chichester, and he does not seem to know what it means to 'take the piss.' I am going to deduce he is not British. I am also going to deduce they are not rich. Margaret's pearls are fakes. Real pearls are not flawless. God does not make flawless things."

"So who are they and what are they doing here?"

"I do not know who they are, but they are definitely here for money. They knew Lasciva was rich and brought tools to break into a safe they had assumed would be here. When Willie told me that Lasciva had been robbed, I thought it might have been a hidden safe. With the limited opportunities afforded them, it appears they have settled for the priceless armor which they have hidden somewhere. How these criminal masterminds thought they would sell it is a mystery to which Holmes himself would surrender."

"Do you think they killed him?"

"I am not sure what to tell you, my friend."

"Right, right, you don't know. Then I suppose I shouldn't ask you what happened to Bernice Lasciva or whose body parts Daniels was dumping in the river or why Daniels shot Ruth or what the purpose of the hellish sounds on the cylinder was."

"No, you should not ask me these questions. Also, do not ask me why Tellum wrote the notes."

Walter put his arm around Rowan. "There is one question I think you can answer."

"By all means."

"What does APC stand for?"

"American Poison Control."

"We need to work on your social life, my friend."

"I am a detective, Williams. I need to know about the latest developments and trends in poison. Arsenic and strychnine are oldfangled."

"Every year you attend this conference?"

"Yes."

"It must be a lively bunch at the annual APC conference."

At that moment, Margaret's head fell on the horn and woke everyone in the car with a start. They spilled out into the dawn with the weary joy of sleep-deprived survival.

Willie seemed particularly upbeat. "Well, don't this beat all. We made it."

The group approached the manor and gingerly stepped through what used to be the front door. The staircase had collapsed in the fire. Water covered the floor and sharp, splintered pieces of wood soaked in it. Sections of the priceless artwork lay strewn about. Rain drizzled lightly through the hole in the roof and the manor stank of masculine mildew.

Ruth was still wearing Walter's suit coat. She held her bloodied arm. "I should make some breakfast. I suppose I'm technically still the hostess."

"Nonsense." Manory ripped off the shards of his shredded suit. "Could everyone work together and lay out some food? I will take Ruth into the library and tend to her arm."

She nodded and dragged herself into the room. Rowan took the cylinder from the upended phonograph and pocketed it. He yanked the ice tongs from the table, sat next to Ruth, and began to inexpertly remove tiny pieces of shrapnel from her arm.

"You are very lucky. Mr. Daniels appears to be a terrible shot. He missed Walter completely and only grazed your flesh." Rowan held up a decanter. "This will hurt you but it will hurt the bacteria more." He poured vodka over her wound.

Ruth bit her lip and held her breath. "It feels better than it tastes."

"What happened after you went to bed?"

"I didn't go to bed. I put on my gown and sat up staring at the door. How could I sleep?"

"You did not have to sleep. You could have just stayed in your room. Apparently it is a very difficult thing to do."

"After a few minutes, there was a knock. I know you said not to open for anyone, but it was Paul. He's a nervous man by nature, but last night he was crazed. He said that Willie had killed Robert." She stared directly into Rowan's eyes. "He said you had told him that. Is that true?"

"I only wished to assure Daniels that he was not a suspect. Never let a suspect know what you are thinking."

"I'll keep that in mind." Ruth took the vodka from Rowan's hand and swigged it. "I don't mean to sound ungrateful detective, but if you suspected Paul of murder, why did you leave us alone with him?"

"There was no reason for him to attack any of you. Quite frankly, I am puzzled as to why he would go after the secretary of Mr. Lasciva. How did you end up in the river?"

"He asked me to come downstairs. When I refused he pulled out the gun. He must have taken it from the billiard room when no one was looking. He tied my hands together and gagged me. It wasn't a fun walk, I can tell you that." She bit a small strip of skin from her pinky. "He led me outside to somewhere in the forest. I'm not sure where, but it was deep into the trees. I lay there for a long time. I thought about getting up and running, but I was too scared. I would have probably walked into the river."

"Did you hear a gunshot?"

"I don't know what I heard. I just waited and hoped. Finally, he came and untied me. His face was…"

Rowan didn't look at her. "Wide-eyed? Astonished?"

"Mad. He took me to the river. I knew he was going to kill me and dump my body, so I shoved him and made a run for it. The gun fired three times. I felt the bullet hit my arm the third time. That's when I fell in."

"I am glad you are still with us."

"So am I."

"How do you feel now?"

"Hungry."

They entered the kitchen to find that breakfast had been served. An enormous plate of dried venison sat in the middle of the table along with several jugs of vodka.

Rowan pulled a chair for Ruth and leaned against the wall, admiring the view. Their hair was disheveled, their clothes stuck to their bodies, and their faces were haggard with rough-looking skin.

*The façade of civilization is razor thin. Look at them, tearing into the meat. Margaret seems even more natural. This is probably the first time Willie has sat at the table. And Charles…*

Rowan's hands shook uncontrollably in clenched fists at the thought of Charles. He did his best to hide it.

Willie said, "Aren't you going to sit down, Mr. Manory?"

"I was just thinking that we should get out of these clothes."

Walter spat out a cherry pit. "I don't know if you've noticed the staircase, boss. No one is getting upstairs."

"There are lots of dress shirts and trousers in Lasciva's closet. If

231

they are still dry, we may as well put them to good use."

"They might be a bit big for the ladies," said Margaret.

"When in Rome, Mrs. Lasciva." He stood directly behind the seated Charles. "I was hoping you would accompany me."

Charles stopped chewing the deer. "What for?"

"To help me carry the clothes."

He looked to Margaret. "Sure. I'd be happy to help."

The stench from Lasciva's drenched corpse filled the office. His head had turned a bluish white.

Rowan headed straight for the desk and searched for any remaining tobacco. There was only enough left for one, terribly meager cigarette.

Charles stood like a man who had spoken out of turn. "Oh God. The smell."

Rowan rolled the tobacco as best he could. "Who are you?"

"I'm afraid I don't understand."

"I am being as reasonable as I can under the circumstances and I have not had any nicotine for a long time. Who are you?"

"I'm Charles."

Rowan lunged forward and backhanded him across the face, but then immediately recoiled. "I'm sorry." He lit the cigarette and puffed. A large pocket of air inside the paper caused its entirety to burn, singeing his hand. "Damn it!

Charles stood, frozen in disbelief. "Detective, I—"

"I do not care about the armor. Do you hear me? I do not care. I need to know who you are. If you do not tell me, I will use every means at my disposal to ruin your life. If I have to lie to the police or plant evidence, I will. My guess is that your resources are limited and when the real police get a hold of you, the thin veneer of your story will crack. If you just tell me now, I can help you and your wife get back home reasonably unscathed."

The boyish man held his face where Rowan had smacked him.

"Please, Charles."

Charles took a deep breath. "Margie and I, we live in California. We do small time cons. I mean, nobody ever gets hurt. I'd never kill anyone."

"I know. How did you know about Lasciva's nephew?"

"We met him on the beach. He was drunk and just spilled his guts. Margie liked his accent. She thought it was the bee's knees. He told us he had a rich uncle in Mississippi and he was probably in line for lots of money. She came up with the idea that we could help him for a small fee. We find his uncle and he would give us a share. There were no ill intentions." He turned to the side and saw Lasciva's head next to him. Charles convulsed.

"What happened to the real Charles Lasciva?"

He caught his breath. "That's the crazy part. I swear to you we didn't do anything. He died. He came to our place and slept on the sofa and in the morning he was dead. We didn't know what to do. There was a dead English hobo on our sofa. Margie checked his pockets and we found his identification and a diary with information about his family. Margie's an actress and she can pull off the accent."

Rowan shrugged. "Perhaps just barely."

"We dumped the body in the ocean."

"What did you do with the armor?"

"We had to get something for our trouble. It's down the road, just before the bridge. She figured we could pick it up later."

"Was the ax in the room?"

"It was gone. I swear it. We would have taken it too."

Rowan stood firm for a moment, thinking it through. "Fine."

"Fine?"

"Yes, fine. Let us get the clothing. Oh…" He paused. "What is your name, anyway?"

"Chuck. You can still call me Charles, I guess."


The sextet sat around the table in some of the finest dress shirts money could buy. Five of them ate and drank. Rowan leaned back in his chair and listened. His face wore a lackluster smile while his mind drifted. He saw a euphoric mania take over the table.

Willie held up his index finger and bent it all the way back, eliciting squeamish cries from the table. "It's the only talent I have."

Margaret's hair frizzed in every conceivable direction and her cheek bones seemed higher than before. "There must be a carnival that would pay you for that. 'Willie Aikes: the human…' I don't even know what you would call that."

"Double-jointed."

"Willie Aikes: the double-jointed freak." Her laughter took control of her body and she hit her hand on the table a little too vigorously.

Charles said, "I think you've had too much vodka, dear."

Walter laughed. "I get it. Vodka. Deer. That's good."

Margaret stood up and spread her shoulders wide. "Reality is my vice. Drink is my only defense."

Charles applauded.

"I don't get that one," said Willie.

"It's a bit of dialogue from a play I was in. Charles came to see it. That's how we met."

Walter shot Rowan a knowing grin.

"I wasn't even an actress. It was some rinky-dink company and my girlfriend begged me to try out. I think the director fancied me."

Willie's smile grew large enough to show a missing molar in the back of his mouth. "What was the play?"

"That's the best part. *Ladies Night in a Turkish Bath*. I had to wear a skimpy bathing suit for the duration of the play, two whole hours."

Rowan eyed her sourly. *That is an American play, you half-wit.*

She continued. "Of course, Charles came to see it."

Charles beamed at his wife. "I do so love the theater."

"He waited for me at the back door and asked me out. Nine times out of ten I would say no but something told me to say yes."

Ruth held her hands together under her chin. "So romantic."

Walter raised his cup. "Job well done, old chap."

Margaret pointed to Ruth. "Robert said you did some acting, too."

Ruth gave an exasperated look. "It was nothing to write home about. I was bored and I answered a local advertisement."

Willie raised his brows. "Miss Martice, what plays did you do?"

"You wouldn't know them. I was in lots of silly farces. I usually played the romantic interest who never said anything important. I did do one murder mystery though. Do you know *The Bat?*"

Everyone shook their head except Rowan who had checked out of this communal affair. *Pure poppycock. A drivel piece of writing. I solved it before the intermission.*

"It was diverting. I got to play Cornelia Van Gorder."

"Now that is quite the name," said Walter.

"She was a fun character. At one point in the play she fires a gun.

That was neat. I also tricked the murderer and helped catch him."

Rowan stood and crossed to the open side of the cabinet and entered the passageway. He looked into the darkness and remembered the monkey from his dream.

*Of course. But…*

He scowled and walked through the dining room into the hall without excusing himself.

"That's a beaten man," said Willie.

Walter shrugged. "I don't think this weekend turned out so well."

"Really?" Margaret laughed. "What went wrong? I hope it wasn't something I said?"

Ruth stood up. "Excuse me." Her throbbing feet carried her down the hallway. A cloud of smoke came from the porch and passed through the door-less frame ahead. Rowan was enjoying one of Lasciva's cigars.

The detective sensed Ruth's presence, but his back remained to the manor. "I am not really a fan of cigars, but I suppose they will do in a pinch." He turned to regard her. "I forgot to thank you for saving my life."

"If you hadn't jumped into the river to save me I wouldn't have had the opportunity. So, it is I who must thank you." She sat on the window ledge and watched the smoke stick to his head. "Do you think we're going to make it?"

"I do not know. It will be a long time, four or five days. Hopefully someone saw the fire."

The sleeves of Lasciva's dress shirt almost doubled the lengths of Ruth's arms and she played with the frills. "Are you sad, Rowan?"

"I am not sad. I am disappointed."

"You wanted to catch Daniels?"

He chomped the cigar with his teeth and then suckled it with his peeling lips. "I am afraid that this case will be my second consecutive failure. I had never failed before. Not only will I not solve the case, but the crime scene has been erased by God. Perhaps he does not want me to solve it."

"You didn't solve your last case?"

"Oh no, I did. I simply made a terrible error in judgment." When he stopped speaking she extended her hands, palms up. "We have plenty of time. I'm willing to listen, unless it's something you'd rather not share."

The drizzle grew into steady rain.

"A man named Martin Brent was strangled in his office. The police had worked on the investigation for over a week and their progress was nonexistent. Martin's wife, Agatha, hired me. Walter and I were in Agatha's home, asking some questions. We were sitting in the living room. Martin's brother, Tommy, was there. Agatha was holding her two-month-old baby."

"They had a child?"

"Yes, it was the worst kind of tragedy. Neither children nor pets make decisions for themselves. They are helpless. At one point during our visit, Williams began discussing baseball with Tommy. It was so much like Williams to do that, to discuss something inappropriate, something that had nothing to do with the topic at hand. He happened to mention that his favorite player on the Cubs was Riggs Stephenson. Tommy Brent replied that Riggs was the tractor company his brother had bought out before he died. This was a horrendous error on Tommy Brent's part. No one knew about this deal. The sale was proposed and made over the phone in Martin's office just before his death."

"How random."

"Out of left field, one could say."

"Why would one say that?"

"As Williams later informed me, Stephenson is a left fielder."

"I don't know anything about baseball."

"Neither do I. Regardless, the case was solved because of Williams's inane discussion of baseball. It is his great talent. He has a sixth sense for using triviality to reveal hidden truths."

"So, what was the problem?"

"The problem was I confronted Tommy Brent right then and there. He had a gun."

"You didn't know?"

Rowan's expression turned cold. "I did not. However, that is entirely of no consequence. It was my fault. You show your cards when you are certain the hand is won."

"What happened?"

"Brent pointed the gun at me. I was sure those were my last moments and I accepted it. I was wrong. He shot Agatha and the baby instead. Then he smiled at me, turned the gun on himself, and fired."

"I'm so sorry."

"I think he knew it was worse than killing me. That is why he smiled. It was the most horrible smile I have ever seen."

"It must be a terrible strain to carry that weight on your shoulders."

"It is one of the reasons I came here. I needed to get away, and it is not as if I had clients beating down my door after such a fiasco."

"What are the other reasons you came here?"

"My mother."

"Your mother? Did she order you to come here?"

Rowan trembled. "She too had a great disappointment in her life. It was also a shortcoming in her profession. There was a young girl who was assaulted. My mother tried to help her, but she failed. The girl was murdered."

"Has she forgiven herself?"

"She never did. They found her dead in a car. Her wrists were slit. No one knew why she had done it. I prayed it was not something I had done. It is because of this case that I now know. The girl's death preyed on my mother's conscience just as Agatha's death preys on mine."

"You thought you could come here and fix it?"

"It was foolish."

"It's admirable."

He moved next to Ruth. "I know what happened."

"You do?"

Lightning struck in the distance.

"I do. Strike that. I..." He began to pace in short strides across the porch. "I am missing one piece of the puzzle. It is the first piece I considered. That is the frustrating part. Everything makes sense except for Robert Lasciva. If I knew what he was doing, then I would know everything. I could be sure. Is he laughing at me from beyond the grave? Why? Surely he knows what happened to him. Surely he knows he was killed. Nothing about him makes any sense!" Rowan stopped pacing and noticed Ruth's worried look. "Did Robert ever tell you how he got the scar on his back?"

She shook her head. "No. I assumed it was from some kind of accident."

The breathless exhaustion from the night before began to fester in Rowan's chest. "Pardon me, Ruth." Rowan walked back into the manor, down the hall, and entered the office. For a brief moment he stood still, frozen by the past.

Without any evident build up, he slammed both fists on the desk and let loose with a scream that caused his lungs to ache. The cuckoo came out to mock him and he fell to his knees on the damp floor. Walter entered the room and leaned beside him.

"Manory, get a grip."

"No, Williams."

"I think at this point we should concentrate on survival. Pneumonia is going to rear its ugly head. Let's focus on getting off this blasted ridge. We can worry about the case later."

"I will never move on until it is solved. It will haunt me forever. The past keeps getting bigger and bigger. Soon it will be all that is left of me."

The rain crashed through the ceiling and spattered against the floor.

Willie entered the office looking concerned. "Is everything okay, Mr. Manory?"

Rowan turned red. "Yes. I am sorry, Willie. This is unacceptable behavior."

"Trust me, I understand, sir. It's perfectly reasonable," said Willie.

Walter put his hand on Rowan's shoulder and grinned. "Willie's right. I mean, is there etiquette for this kind of situation?"

Rowan stared daggers. "Third fucking time!"

Walter jerked his hand from Rowan's shoulder. "Rowan, it was a joke."

Manory wept.

Willie said, "I'll check and see if we have any more of those cherries you both like. It's too bad we aren't at my brother's. He gets 'em fresh off the tree. Jerry loves his cherries."

"What did you say?" asked Walter.

"I said my brother Jerry loves his cherries."

"Oh. I thought you said, 'Cherry loves his cherries.' It would be quite the coincidence if your brother was named Cherry."

"Yes sir, I guess it would be."

Willie left the room and Walter turned to find that Rowan had risen from the wet oak floor. His face had that look of astonishment.

"What is it, old man?"

Rowan walked forward and kissed Walter on the lips. He jumped into the air, nearly kicking Lasciva's head. "How could I be so stupid? Oh my God!"

"I... You..."

"Williams, say 'cherry.'"

"Cherry."

"Now say 'Jerry.'"

"Jerry."

"Now say them together."

"Cherry Jerry."

"Now repeat them again and again."

"Cherry Jerry, Cherry Jerry, Cherry Jerry—"

"Faster, Williams."

Walter did as he was instructed and began laughing. "Yes, the 'j' sound becomes the 'ch' sound. That was my initial confusion, the slight difference between the voiced and unvoiced consonants."

"Now say 'choke,'" said Rowan with his smug smile.

# CHAPTER 16

# REVELATION

The vague hint of sun had given way to a dingy, cerulean light. Lightning flashed in the sky once again. Rain poured down from the exposed roof. Manory paced in the hall, his shoes squelching on the floor. He replayed the events one last time. The fog lifted from the puzzle. Every piece fit. Everything was crystal.

He entered the library where everyone was gathered at his behest. Willie and Ruth sat on one sofa, Charles and Margaret on the second, and Walter took the third.

Charles spoke. "What's in the bag?"

Manory dropped the burlap sack on the floor. It hit with the force of a wet sponge. He paced the room in silence, as if winding a stem.

When he felt the tension in the room had peaked, he began.

"Ladies and gentleman, three savage murders took place last night, the latter two seemingly inexplicable. Jack Tellum was poisoned. Robert Lasciva was decapitated, and a third man, a mystery man, was stabbed. To top it off, Bernice Lasciva performed a magic trick and disappeared from a locked room. I shall now reveal how and why it was done."

The detective bristled with alacrity and gesticulated with every word. The pent-up frustration had vanished and in its place grew a manic energy. He held the bridge of his nose between his fingers and cracked it back into place.

"The crux of this case eluded me and yet, it was so simple. There were two cases to solve. I chose the wrong one."

Willie stood up. "Mr. Manory, we're all tired. Can't you just—"

"William."

"It's Willie, sir."

"Sit."

Willie sat back down.

Manory audibly cleared his throat. "I was hired by Robert Lasciva because he had received a threat, a very strange threat. He would be killed during his party by one of his guests." Manory curled his lips. "An old friend."

No one knew where he was heading. Ruth bit into bleeding fingers. Willie leaned his heavy frame on the arm of the sofa. Charles kept swallowing air. Margaret pressed her knees against her chest. Every nerve in the room was naked.

"When I was first contacted by Lasciva, I was confused. Why me? Why would Robert Lasciva hire me? To answer this question, we must go back twenty years. During the Chicago winter of 1907, Robert Lasciva and his crony Jack Tellum raped and stabbed a seven-year old girl."

Manory met and briefly held each suspect's gaze.

*The eyes reveal so much more than the mouth.*

"The girl's name was Irene Roberts. Her mother Dorothy had begun a casual affair with Lasciva. When Dorothy came home and discovered the unspeakable things they had done... Well. The guilt she felt after leaving her only daughter alone and introducing these monsters into her life was too much for her to bear. She elected to take her own life and leapt out the window to her death."

Ruth's mouth crumpled. "Did the police arrest them?"

"No. They had plenty of evidence. Several people saw Lasciva and Tellum leaving the building, and Tellum had been wounded by the child. Irene had the nickname 'mouse' because of her buckteeth. They matched a mark on Tellum's finger, presumably inflicted during his attack on her. Paul Daniels used his influence to deflect justice for his friends. The case was buried. No one cared. That is, almost no one."

"How is this connected to you, Mr. Manory?" asked Margaret.

Manory nodded. "My mother was a member of the police. During the course of the investigation she developed a relationship with the young girl, an emotional attachment. When it became apparent that Lasciva would go free, she was understandably devastated."

Manory froze for a moment as flurries from the past came to the threshold. He pushed them away.

"In any event, she felt it her duty to punish Robert Lasciva in some way and opted to reveal his perversion to people far more powerful than he. Lasciva knew this. He knew that Ellen Manory had ruined him. I am sure it will surprise no one to learn that Robert Lasciva could hold a grudge. Enter Rowan Manory. Lasciva read about my recent difficulties. His remaining connections in Chicago probably helped him with my exact whereabouts. And so, I was invited to his birthday party for the purpose of discovering his would-be-killer, a would-be-killer who did not exist. No one had threatened Robert Lasciva."

"What about the letter?" asked Charles.

"During our investigation, Williams and I discovered that Jack Tellum had penned the threat."

Walter raised a finger. "Umm…"

Manory sighed. "Williams discovered that Jack Tellum had penned the threat."

"Does that mean Mr. Tellum was involved in Robert's murder?" asked Margaret.

"No, it does not. Jack Tellum wrote the threat by direct order. Robert Lasciva told him to write it."

"Why?" asked Ruth. "What purpose would it serve?"

Manory stopped pacing for a moment. "Revenge." He began again. "Let us examine what was supposed to happen. Lasciva's plan was to make himself and his aunt disappear, to vanish without a trace. Jack Tellum would then plant a note for me, the same note we retrieved from his pocket. It would specify that two people had been murdered: Lasciva and his aunt. Eventually Jack himself would disappear, followed by Paul Daniels, and in the morning, I would find the second note. In total, the notes to me specified four gone without a single body as proof: Robert, Bernice, Jack, and Paul. Using a secret passage as their conduit, they could have remained missing. It seems to have been some kind of murder mystery theatre for Lasciva's own twisted amusement. He even told me that he was a fan of such stories. He must have had a grand time plotting out the details."

"The cylinder with the ghost noises," said Walter.

"Yes. Imagine it, Williams: you and I searching the upstairs when suddenly the howling of ghosts would come from below. And do not forget the will. With so many in the manor in line for his fortune, there would be a bevy of suspects."

"How would Mr. Lasciva disappear?" asked Willie.

"His plan was to hide inside the armor within the locked case. We would break down the door and find no one, nothing but an empty office. Bernice picked a fight with Ruth in order to highlight her seclusion with her nephew. It was important that I knew the two of them were alone in the room together. The movements must have been choreographed with Tellum and Daniels beforehand. The second note, which, like the first, we found before its scheduled appearance, would have eventually led me to the secret passageway and my demise. It was not enough to kill me. No, no, he had to fool me as well." Manory motioned toward Charles and Margaret. "Perhaps he had a similar fate in store for the two of you."

Margaret grabbed Charles's hand. "What would he have against us?"

Charles turned to his wife. "He knows."

"I believe Robert Lasciva knew as well. Something tells me that he would not take kindly to scam artists trying to steal from him."

Manory stopped pacing in front of the window and spoke with his back to the room. "Because of my gargantuan ego, I like to think that I would have solved the case before my untimely death. However, we shall never know because of the wildest monkey wrench, the most poetic taste of one's own medicine anyone could possibly imagine. I have seen the swallowing of jewels, a puffer fish poisoning, and a woman strangled with her own cat, but I have never seen anything like this."

The thunder boomed and echoed along the ridge.

Manory turned round to see Walter with his hand raised.

"Just ask, Williams."

"I don't mean to rush you, boss, but what happened to Bernice Lasciva? I think that's what everyone is really waiting for."

His smug smile reappeared. "Ahh yes, Bernice Lasciva. It was her duty to lock the case after Robert positioned himself inside. It would not occur to me that he would be in the armor if the glass case were locked. Tellum or Daniels could free him later. Unfortunately for our gangster friend, his aunt had a radically different interpretation of the plan. After he put on the body of the suit, she knocked him down. He lay on the floor, helpless in a heavy suit of armor. With a whack of the ax, she then severed his head and placed it in the helmet for good measure."

Willie shook his head. "No, sir. She couldn't do that. That woman could barely make it down the stairs."

"And yet she did."

Ruth took her thumb out of her mouth. "Where did she go?"

Manory seemed puzzled by the question. "She left the room."

The library erupted in vehement protest and Manory patted his hands down to quiet them.

"Patience. I will get there. I promise. So, we know that Paul Daniels poisoned Tellum. Using antifreeze as his agent of choice, Paul made it a point to drink the poisoned panther piss in front of Charles and Margaret. This would naturally divert suspicion. What poisoner would drink his own concoction? By partaking in the drinking of vodka, he effectively tempered the properties that eventually turned Tellum's insides to bloody mush."

Manory was gaining steam. He twirled and continued talking.

"Why? Why would Daniels do such a thing to his friend? It was because he was working with Bernice Lasciva. When we burst through the door, the key was not inside."

Ruth objected. "But you saw it through the keyhole."

"No. I assumed. There is that terrible word. Our eyes and ears tell us things that we expect to see and hear. I assumed I saw the key, but it was not there. I saw something else. When we broke in the office, our eyes naturally focused on the decapitated, armored corpse. Paul Daniels took this moment to slip in the door key. He then turned and," Manory paused for effect, "he was shocked. He did not know the savage fury that Bernice had in store for Robert. Twice he exclaimed his surprise. 'His *head* is cut off!' I imagine for him, the deaths of Robert and Jack were business. For Bernice, they were personal. Daniels had expected to see Lasciva's throat slit or perhaps some other knife wound. That crazy old woman cut off his head and put it in a helmet."

Walter spoke up. "Did Bernice hide in the secret passage?"

Manory only smiled. "While you and I made our excursion into the woods, Daniels and Bernice met in the passage. Once again, different plans had been made, very different plans."

"Did he kill her?" Ruth leaned forward.

Manory froze. The implications hit him. This presentation was for him, a triumph of his prowess. The cost, however, had not occurred to him.

*Steady, old man.*

"One of the most baffling elements of this case was the note to Lasciva. Chip chop, chip chop. These were the very words of Irene Roberts, quoted from her favorite nursery rhyme. I thought a lot about Irene as we drove here. I thought about the terrible wrong that had been done to her. She disappeared years ago. A local child murderer had confessed to killing her, but the body was never found. I did not believe for a second that this man had killed her. All I could imagine was that poor girl being murdered by the most monstrous wretch anyone could imagine, a man whose appetite could only be whetted by the most Sadean acts. But now here she was, directly referenced in the threat. Was she speaking from beyond the grave? Or was she waiting in the night, ready to strike?" Manory circled the room, his heart beating confidently. He stopped in front of Ruth.

"Mowshen."

She looked up with steely features. All the kindness dropped from her face.

"I should have known when I heard Bernice's accent. You see, I went to visit Alice Schmidt before I came here. It was Alice's voice you used. She misses you terribly. She thinks about you every day. I have seen *The Bat*. Cornelia Van Gorder is a wonderful character. You and I both know she is an old woman. I imagine the role taught you quite a bit about make-up, wigs, and the way old women walk. You convinced Robert you could take on the role of Bernice Lasciva. It was a bravura performance, Irene. While I toured the house, you went upstairs and got into character. Why would I not believe Bernice existed? Everyone vouched for her."

Willie Aikes rose from the sofa and stood, leaving Irene alone. "The two of you were never together."

An awful feeling came over Walter. "We heard them arguing."

Manory said, "You argued with yourself while slipping out of costume and putting on the black dress. Robert played along, still unaware of the danger. I tried to warn him. I told him about the nursery rhyme. But no, he could not imagine it. In the doorway of the office, he asked you who had added the nursery rhyme to the letters. You told him that Tellum had done it. It must have been quite a rush to know you would kill Lasciva after all these years, hence the very real emotion you displayed."

Irene's dug-up fury twitched the muscles of her face.

"It was you arguing with Daniels on the porch. There was no one in the window when I saw the silhouettes. Perhaps he was getting cold feet. He needed a slap in the face. I noticed how red his face was when I arrived, but putting two and two together is getting harder and harder for me these days. You never had an affair with Lasciva. You did not even know where the scar was on his body. But you did have an affair with a fellow in Clarksdale. While Daniels was showing Walter the painting, you slipped through the passage just as Lasciva had planned. Paul made sure to keep Walter's eyes on the painting and away from the other side of the hall. Robert unlocked the door for you after he put on the armor. You killed him for what he had done to you and what he had done to your mother. You even placed your gum on the keyhole. Later, you made sure to tell me to look through it so I would know the key was in place. After the deed had been done, you took Bernice's clothes, walked out the door, locked it and went back through the passage and rushed to the library doorway. It was just in time to be seen by Williams. You slipped Daniels the key while no one was looking. Tellum realized something was wrong. It was far too late, but he tried to tell me the evening had been a joke. Once again, my ears assumed. You took out the gun for Paul to retrieve and you helpfully reminded me that Tellum was choking and not joking. In the office, Paul dutifully removed the gum and stuck it under the table like the jackass he was."

Four of the mouths in the room were open in stunned silence.

"Two down and one to go, chip chop, chip chop. When you had a chance to kill Daniels, you took it. You stabbed him in the passageway with the missing knife from the kitchen. Then you chopped him into pieces and sought to wash his body away in order to deflect any suspicion. A forever-missing Daniels would naturally cause him to be the prime suspect."

Walter stood. "Now wait a minute. I saw Paul Daniels in the forest. I am positive."

Manory's voice rose. "I have no doubt, my friend. You did see Paul Daniels. How did you describe him, with a look of shock and disorientation? It is the same shock and disorientation that is now permanently etched on the face of Robert Lasciva!" He plucked Lasciva's head from the sack and held it in front of his own.

The day turned absolutely dark and lightning controlled the sky. Manory threw the head on the ground. "In the dark, in the distance, you saw Daniels's severed head in front of the raincoat and you assumed it was him." The detective turned back to Irene. "If the last sack had been taken by the river no one would ever know, but I recovered it. I knew there was another dead man. Now you were desperate and you had to make a distraction. Oh yes, there was lots of bravery on display last night. You grazed your own arm with a bullet and then, when we got close, you threw yourself into the river to be saved."

Irene gave a joyless smile.

"The same girl who bit Jack Tellum's thumb in defense all those years ago has finally struck back, your dermatophagia a permanent reminder of that helpless battle. You planned it. How long? You did not kill Lasciva right away, no. Tellum was always near. You began an affair with Paul Daniels and convinced him to betray his friends for control of the business. The serendipity of this party must have been amusing for you. The murdered man would provide proof of Bernice's existence and give his own murderer an alibi. And of course, you worded the notes. The secretary created the threat and the clues. Tellum dutifully wrote them out. Your signature is on every paper in this house, so it would not do to have your handwriting on the notes. Chip chop, chip chop. The sign was right in front of his goddamned face. Alas, you did not know our connection. The same woman who tried to help you twenty years ago, her son would show up on your night of vengeance. He would show up, thinking of you in the back of his mind. My gut told me you would be here. It was right."

Irene slowly stood and walked graceless and bowlegged to the center of the library. Everyone in the room stared at her. Rowan looked into the eyes that had once been familiar, but were now those of a stranger.

"Would you be surprised to know that I can't even remember your mother?"

"She never forgot you."

"I ran away because I wanted to forget my past. Every winter

257

brought me nightmares and fits of rage the likes of which you can't begin to imagine. You're wrong about one thing. None of it was planned. One day I got on a bus. I didn't even know where it was going. I thought someone would surely come looking for me. But then a funny thing happened, Rowan. No one did. I didn't know why that man confessed to my murder and I didn't care. It's just one of life's funny coincidences. The bus took me to Urbana. There's a little art commune there. They don't ask many questions. I did theatre, wrote, painted, anything not to think about the past. I came here to help with the flood, just like I told you. My past followed me, though. It knew. It knew I would come here. Paul said Lasciva's name once, and all my anger came back. I congratulate you, Mr. Manory. I'm happy for you, I truly am. It must be a great relief to know that you are still a brilliant detective. But a question arises. What now?"

Manory was still breathing heavily from his speech. "Now? Now we will wait until rescue arrives, and then you will be turned over to the authorities to face the consequences of your crimes."

Walter mouthed the word no.

"You will turn me in? For killing that man? You will seek to avenge *his* death? I could have killed you in the passageway. I could have killed Walter by the river. I could have killed these liars. I didn't. I saved your life. I killed the men who destroyed mine! My mother—" Tears ran down her face, but her cold expression remained. "If I go to jail for killing them, they win again. Don't you see that?"

"Irene, I promise you I will do everything in my power to aid in your defense. Your situation will be seen as extraordinary. You have suffered so much. Any jury would take it into consideration."

"Take it into consideration? I can't believe this!" Her large eyes beaded with tears. "The law failed me twenty years ago and now it will punish me! Rowan, do you believe in justice?"

Manory defiantly stared down Irene. He grimaced.

# CHAPTER 17

# CHICAGO 1928

Walter stared at the number with grim determination. His gaze switched to the new device on his desk. A large, built-up breath came out of his body.

"I'm sorry, Mr. Reynolds. You'll have to explain this one more time. What does this number do?"

The portly Reynolds beamed with assuredness. "Mr. Williams, this is your number."

"Michigan 6-5216 is my number?"

"Yes, but you notice how the first two letters are capitalized. People only need to dial MI and then the numbers. I explained all of this to Mr. Manory."

"I can appreciate that, but as Mr. Manory's assistant, I'll be using the phone far more often than he will. I need to understand it." He counted the numbers in his head. "That's seven numbers. Do people have to tell the switchboard operator all seven numbers?"

"That's the beauty of it, Mr. Williams. They don't have to connect through an operator. They can call you directly. It's called an automatic exchange. If you dial someone with their own number, you can skip the operator too."

"But I like the switchboard operators. Some of the best conversations I've ever had were with those women. I'm good friends with some of them."

Aaron Reynolds had been busting his hump all day and the willful ignorance of this curious fellow was trying his patience. "If you want, you can still go through the operator. All you have to do is dial zero."

"I dial zero for the operator?"

"Now you're on the trolley."

"Why don't I dial 'O' for operator? Wouldn't that make more sense? Zero doesn't stand for anything."

Reynolds looked at Walter quizzically.

"All right, never mind. How do I work the telephone?"

"It's the same principle as the candlestick phone, except the receiver and the transmitter are connected. It's so much more comfortable."

Walter picked up the phone and held it to his ear. "There's some ghastly noise."

"I already explained that. That's called a dial tone. It means the phone is ready for you to dial the number."

Walter stood up and walked a few steps. "It feels odd. I don't know what to do with my other hand."

"I'm sure you'll be able to figure something out." Reynolds checked his pocket watch. "I have to get down to the firehouse. We've installed a new line there as well. If you have any other questions, you can call me."

"Maybe I will. I can dial zero for operator and she'll still connect us, right?"

"That's right."

Walter saw Reynolds to the door and sat with his new technology again.

*Everything changes.*

Rowan came into the office and kicked the snow off his boots. He laid a box of chocolates on the desk. "You look troubled, Williams."

"Everything changes but nothing gets any better. Have you ever noticed that?"

"Yes. I believe people call it, 'the future.'" Rowan pointed to the new device. "Is this it?"

"Yes, this is our new telephone along with our new number."

"Magnificent." Rowan picked up the phone and put the handset next to his ear. He jerked it away, looking startled.

Walter pushed down the hook switch. "Dial tone."

"Hmmm." Rowan put it back against his ear and balanced it with his shoulder. He paced in front of the desk with contentment. "Look, Walter. I can talk on the phone while I use both hands. Think of how much more we can get done."

Manory Investigations had slowly picked up business since the August weekend at Lasciva Manor. A high-profile case in November had brought good publicity and a newly rediscovered trust from the public. Now it was January and the company's change in fortune had made the Chicago snowstorms more picturesque and less threatening.

Rowan settled into his chair. He flipped open the front page of the newspaper. The top story was the execution of Charles Shader along with the trendy debate about capital punishment. Rowan brooded over the negativity of the news.

*Surely there are positive things to report in a city of three million people.*

The detective sensed the expectant stare of Walter Williams and folded down a corner of the paper. "Do you want something, Williams?"

"Yeah, I want to know what the doctor said."

Rowan smirked. "I am as fit as a fiddle, just as I had predicted. Doctor Paulson was very complimentary. He said my blood pressure was so

264

good he could sell it. The man is quite witty."

"Well you have to keep going for regular check-ups. Don't simply assume you're in good health after one visit."

"Once I re-established my prowess as a detective, my mind was healed. The body obeys the mind, Williams."

"So you've finally put the Tommy—"

"Ahh ahh ahh! We do not say his name anymore."

"You've put that awful case that we will never mention again behind you?"

"Absolutely." Rowan opened the newspaper again. "Did you know the Thames flooded last week? Fourteen are dead. According to journalists the world is a terrible place to live."

"England doesn't even know what a flood is. How many died in our flood?"

"Five hundred is the estimate."

"That's all?"

"You wanted more?"

"No, of course not. It just seemed so much worse. We were there. You do remember, don't you? Or have you chosen to erase that case from your mind too?"

"If it makes you feel any better, hundreds of thousands lost their homes."

"Come now, Manory."

"There was one billion dollars in damage. I would bet England cannot even fathom the concept of a billion."

"I liked you more when you were ill and serious."

Rowan smiled and lifted the paper.

Walter forced a cough. "Is there any news about Irene Roberts?"

The paper came down once more. "Her trial is in March. I have hired the best lawyer I can find and I will testify on her behalf. There is nothing more I can do."

Walter popped a chocolate in his mouth. "I think you could have saved yourself a lot of time and money."

"I am aware of your opinion, Williams."

"I think about her a lot, Manory. I dream about Irene. She's always in the river. I reach for her—"

"But she goes under."

"Yes, but before she does, she begs me for help. Do you have the same dream?"

"No." Rowan put his finger on the front headline. "Yesterday, this Shader fellow was hanged. According to the prison psychologist, he had an awful childhood. His father tortured him daily. Perhaps the law should not have applied to him."

"He killed a warden. Irene killed a murdering, pedophilic gangster.

There's really no comparison."

"We will have to agree to disagree, my friend. These dreams will end when you discover a new obsession."

Walter was not so sure.

A knock came on the office door and Manory instinctively checked his pocket watch. "Ten minutes until office hours are over. I swear our clients wait until the last possible moment just to make sure we do not get home on time. Please, Williams, earn your rubes."

Walter sighed and walked to the door. He thought perhaps the phone technician had forgotten to tell him something important. He opened the door and was startled at the resemblance.

*Bernice.*

Walter's eyes were immediately drawn to the frizzy white hair. She was clad in a dusty black dress. He attempted to ask if he could help her but the exact words evaded his tongue.

"Is Herr Manory in?"

"Yes, he is. Who may I say is—"

"Frau Schmidt." Rowan stood from his desk and made his way to the door. "It is such a pleasure to see you again." He took her by the arm and led her to the chair at his desk. He gave Williams a hard look behind her back.

Walter pulled his hat and coat off the hook. "Well, Manory, I best be off. I'll see you tonight at the Brown Bear. Good day, madam." He hesitated and then walked out, shutting the door behind him.

Rowan bent down and spoke slowly. "Shall I get you something to drink, some tea, perhaps?"

"Nothing, thank you." Despite the agitation of her muscles, Alice's gaze remained steady.

"I have been meaning to pay you a visit, but unfortunately work has been taking all of my time. Criminals never seem to take a holiday." He sat with a warm smile. "How have you been?"

"Mr. Manory, I mean you no offense but I am not here to chat. I do not care about pleasantries or weather."

Rowan took out the inevitable papers and tobacco. He began to absently roll himself a cigarette and flatly said, "I see."

"You promised me if you found out what happened to my mäuschen, you would tell me."

Manory laid the paper and tobacco down. Alice's eyes remained fixed on his face. He stood and turned to the window. The snow silently fell and piled heavily onto the ground like white lead.

*This city is gorgeous if you do not have to live in it.*

# The End

# ABOUT THE AUTHOR

James Scott Byrnside despises writing blurbs about himself. A lifelong love of reading murder mysteries inspired him to attempt writing one. The result is *Goodnight Irene*. He is now hooked. His next novel, *Nemesis*, is scheduled to be released in July of 2019. You can visit him at www.facebook.com/mysterywriting/. He kindly asks that you leave an honest review on Amazon.

Lightning Source UK Ltd.
Milton Keynes UK
UKHW011811060219
336865UK00023B/879/P